Y0-BRS-755

"Marriage? I'm terrified by the mere idea."

Diane laughed. "Wonderful! So am I. Are there any more of those chips?"

Ira looked at the empty bowl and shook his head. "You *are* hungry."

"Yes, I am." Her voice was husky and suddenly the last thing on her mind was food. "What are you going to do about it?"

Ira was unable to resist and he pulled her into his arms. He kissed her, teasing her lower lip with his tongue then biting gently. "You make me lose control...." he murmured.

Diane stepped back and shook her head. "I cooperated."

"Beautifully. I hope you plan to continue."

"I haven't been making any plans, Ira, just letting things happen." *Like you*, she thought.

This time Ira pulled her against him gently, his body taut and hard, his scent a wonderful mixture of soap and musky maleness. "I'm an absolute expert at living by impulse," he whispered in her ear. "If you'd like to try it, you couldn't find a better teacher...."

Joanna Gilpin loves the sea and the peacefulness of traveling afloat. She and her husband, a former commercial fisherman and watercolor artist, built a live-aboard boat and spent fifteen years fishing. As a result, many of her stories, including *Chance It*, are set at sea. The only research she had to do was on the modern-day pirates who are a dangerous threat to yachtsmen in the lower Bahamas.

Joanna is a Florida native who was brought up on the same waterfront property where she now lives. After a successful newspaper career, she turned her hand to romances with equally happy results.

Books by Joanna Gilpin
HARLEQUIN TEMPTATION
163—FIRST MATES
239—A SIMPLE "I DO"

Don't miss any of our special offers. Write to us at the following address for information on our newest releases.

Harlequin Reader Service
P.O. Box 1397, Buffalo, NY 14240
Canadian address: P.O. Box 603,
Fort Erie, Ont. L2A 5X3

Chance It

JOANNA GILPIN

Harlequin Books

TORONTO • NEW YORK • LONDON
AMSTERDAM • PARIS • SYDNEY • HAMBURG
STOCKHOLM • ATHENS • TOKYO • MILAN

Published January 1991

ISBN 0-373-25430-X

CHANCE IT

Copyright © 1991 by Joanna McGauran. All rights reserved.
Except for use in any review, the reproduction or utilization
of this work in whole or in part in any form by any electronic,
mechanical or other means, now known or hereafter invented,
including xerography, photocopying and recording,
or in any information storage or retrieval system, is forbidden without
the permission of the publisher, Harlequin Enterprises Limited,
225 Duncan Mill Road, Don Mills, Ontario, Canada M3B 3K9.

All the characters in this book have no existence outside the
imagination of the author and have no relation whatsoever to
anyone bearing the same name or names. They are not even
distantly inspired by any individual known or unknown to the
author, and all incidents are pure invention.

® are Trademarks registered in the United States Patent and
Trademark Office and in other countries.

Printed in U.S.A.

1

YURI STEPHAN DIED on a cool, late-April day and rumor shook the world of Florida real estate. Yuri, at seventy-eight, was the multimillionaire king of south Florida's market in land and buildings, and rumor had it that his empire was up for grabs. As the day progressed, Yuri's partner, thirty-two-year-old Diane Roberts, calmly announced to the media that she would sell the Stephan interests—all of them and all at once—to the highest bidder.

The announcement was greeted with raised eyebrows and mocking smiles, as well as excitement. No one was surprised that Yuri had signed over his holdings to Ms. Roberts rather than to his already wealthy, grown children—there was always more between the partners than a business relationship. As someone said, perhaps Ms. Roberts should have waited a few days to announce the auction, but who could blame her? Young and reasonably attractive, Diane had been tied down to old Yuri for six years. That was long enough.

On the day after Yuri was buried, in one of the biggest funerals ever held in Miami Beach, Diane visited the soaring, Stephan office building on Biscayne Bay.

She slipped in without fanfare, using the service elevator and going directly to her office, a quietly expensive room done in cool pastels and decorated with growing plants; a bank of windows behind her desk looked out over the sparkling bay and the western shore of Key Biscayne. She planned to stay just long enough to hand over the reins of the business to Henry Wilton, chairman of the board. Waiting, she stood at the windows and watched the boats in the bay through a haze of tears, thinking of Yuri and the past. A gentle touch on her shoulder roused her from reverie.

"You gave him years more," Henry Wilton said softly, "happy years. Stop grieving."

Diane's slender hand covered his. "I know. But he was my rock. My true father. I miss him. I always will." She turned, dashing the tears away and finding a smile. "You're the new CEO, by the way. The boss, until we sort out the best deal. When the sale goes through, I'll recommend that they keep you and the rest of the directors. Yuri knew how to pick men."

The new CEO was fifty-two, medium-sized and gray-haired, with an angular, intelligent face. "He knew how to pick women, too," Henry said. "You've been running this place for four years, Diane. No one could do it better. Why not keep on? Take some time off. A cruise or a trip to Europe. Have a relaxing vacation. But come back to us. We need you."

"That's flattering, Henry, and I appreciate it. You were very thoughtful when I had to take over, and I don't forget things like that. But I won't be back. I may take that cruise, though, or something like it. I could use some playtime."

Wilton regarded her thoughtfully. Except for the slight reddening from her tears she looked fine. She was wearing a loose, white suit, sterling silver earrings and a wide, silver bracelet. Her skin was naturally a warm ivory, her hair a shining sable brown, her eyes a surprising sea blue. But no one would ever call her beautiful. Her mouth was a bit too wide, her narrow, patrician nose marred by a small and crooked hump. On the rounded forehead, just above one eyebrow, was an inch-long, jagged scar that she usually kept hidden with makeup. Henry had once blurted out that both nose and scar could be repaired by plastic surgery. Diane had replied that the faults were part of her life experience and she needed them. Henry had shut up, concluding they didn't bother her. Nothing much did; her expression was always reserved and incredibly calm, even now, when her whole life was changing.

"I still think you're wrong," he said slowly. "I know you. You'll be bored in a month with nothing to do."

Diane leaned back and stared past him. Henry did know her, probably better than anyone else, now that Yuri was gone. He knew, for instance, that she hadn't taken up with Yuri for his money—her father, Harrington Roberts, had inherited an immense fortune, and she was his only child. Henry also knew she socialized with no one except Anna and Paul, Yuri's two children, both older than her by many years. And, Diane admitted to herself, possibly Henry was right. Without some challenge to occupy her mind, she quite likely would get bored. But Yuri, her beloved friend and mentor, had given her her final orders before he died.

"Don't do as I did, do as I say," Yuri had told her. "You won't need your father's money. I've seen to it that you and Anna and Paul will have enough for your lifetimes. So, go forth into the world and look for happiness and adventure. Find a man you can share with." He had frowned at her suddenly sour expression, but he understood. Yuri was the only person in the world who knew exactly what she thought of her chances when it came to romance. And why.

"Listen for once," he had added, grasping her wrist with his wiry, feverish hand. "I know what you're thinking about, but that happened over eight years ago. Forget it—you're no silly kid now, you can judge a man as well as I can. I want you to take chances—to fling yourself into life! Get rid of the corporation and find out what really matters to you. I want to know, now, that when your time comes to die, you can look back and say you've had it all. So promise me!"

Remembering, Diane's face softened. "We're selling, Henry. Actually, I can't change my mind on that. It's something I promised Yuri."

Fling yourself into life. Leaving the building, Diane decided that was easier said than done. Given her habit of strict self-discipline, it might be impossible. But something inside her yearned to find out.

Later she drove along Brickell Drive, considering Henry Wilton's remark about a cruise. Glancing out across shining Biscayne Bay, she turned south. Years ago, she and Yuri had often chartered a yacht for a day and once had hired one for a full month and cruised the Bahamas. But that hadn't lasted long. Yuri had plunged back into his ever-growing business and she had joined in. But she had never forgotten the peaceful solitude of the ocean. It might be a great way to start a new life, and she knew where to look. Along the bay and in the coves were marinas, and in marinas yachts were for sale.

THAT AFTERNOON, Ira Nicholson brought his fifty-seven-foot cruiser *Sea Fever* back from the Bahamas. Long ago, Ira had traded the plush grandeur of fancy yacht clubs for smaller, less formal marinas, and today he picked one of his favorites, the Biscay Yacht Basin, where he was well known. There, slowing the *Sea Fever* to a crawl, he eased along the lines of other boats until he found himself nearly past the only open slip. Alerted by noise, he turned and saw a forty-five-foot Hatteras behind him, coasting up to sneak into the space. Swearing under his breath, he jerked the port engine into reverse, shoved the starboard into forward, and whirled the *Sea Fever*'s imposing bulk broadside to the bow of the smaller boat. Then, as the Hatteras roared into reverse to keep from hitting him, he eased the starboard throttle, coasted backward into the slip and stepped from the cabin to the deck, grabbing lines and tying up. Wind-tousled, tanned and bare except for shorts, he grinned at the red-faced captain glaring at him from the bridge of the other boat.

"Nice try."

"I came damn close to ramming you when you turned that sharp," the other man snarled. "That slip's too small for you, anyway."

"I'm in it," Ira said, and stepped back from the rail to get a good look at the other man. Casual and relaxed, he kept the expression on his bronzed face noncommittal.

On the deck of the forty-five-footer the other man stared back. What he saw was a big, very fit man with sun-streaked, shaggy, brown hair and damned funny-looking eyes, more yellow than brown. Eyes like a tiger's. Struck by a thought, he glanced at the name of the big boat, clamped his jaw shut and began looking for another space. He had heard of this guy and wasn't about to start anything.

Ira, at over six foot and close to a lean two hundred pounds of bone and muscle, had never been known to start a fight—or turn one down. He was a man's man, an anachronism in the 1990s—an avid hunter, fisherman, outdoorsman and tracker. Men told stories about his exploits, including how Nicholson had conquered the problem of staying out of offices and financing a good life in the few and faraway places where a man could still hunt and fish.

It was no more than dumb luck, they said, that he'd stumbled on a way to make an improved, infrared night scope for rifles, and the military of several countries had bought it. Then, after Ira had played around and won a bunch of deep-sea tournaments, he'd marketed a line of sportfishing equipment with his name on it. That had turned into a runaway sales success. And finally, when he really didn't need money anymore, he began earning commissions here and there by occasionally selling one of a new line of yachts. Since they sold for a million or more, the commissions were a nice sideline. The few men who knew him well said that he'd left home when he graduated from high school, and he'd never been to a college or held a steady job; just messed around, while Lady Luck dogged his footsteps.

With the boat secured, Ira leaped to the walkway and made his way, barefoot on the sun-hot concrete, past lockers and sails piled on the ground, past a forest of masts where sailboats gathered in a large flock, past the hot, June odors from garbage-flecked, oily water below and trash barrels spoiling in the sun, and finally arrived at the marina office.

"Ira! You're back!"

He grinned and caught the scantily-clad woman who rose from the desk to throw her arms around his neck. "Hey, Rosie, watch it. I don't want Big John gunning for me."

Rose Thomas kissed his cheek and stepped back. Blonde and cute, dressed in pink shorts and a pink-flowered shirt, she grinned up at him. "If I thought it would make the big ape jealous, I'd do it again. But he doesn't worry, not with those gorgeous gals that flock around when you come home. How do you ever choose between them, Ira?"

Scribbling his name and number on the register, Ira winked. "I let them draw straws. But this time I'm not calling them around. I'm thinking of selling the boat."

"Selling the *Sea Fever*?" Rose sounded aghast. "How could you? That beautiful hulk! Besides, there's no one around here who could afford it. What would you ask? A million?"

He shook his head. "Naw. I've put some hard hours on those diesels and some scratches on the paint. I'd ask maybe eight hundred thousand." He gave her a rueful smile. "And maybe I won't sell at all. I'm having some second thoughts."

"Wait," Rose advised. "See what kind of offers you get. In the meantime, if you need groceries you can borrow my car."

"Thanks."

She let him get to the door before she added: "Shoes, pal. No bare feet allowed in grocery stores."

Ira groaned. "The ads are right. It's different, in the Bahamas."

Rose watched him as he went down the hot walk with his easy stride and gave a tiny sigh. Some men had it, she thought, and some men didn't. Big John had it, at least for her. Ira Nicholson, with those hot, golden eyes and that touch-me body, was loaded with it. It was just as well he'd never married. Chasing other females away would be tiresome.

BY THE TIME Ira made it back to the docks with his bag of fresh fruit and vegetables, the sun had dropped far enough to lay some shade along the walk and across the aft deck of the *Sea Fever*. He opened the insulated, waterproof door below the captain's bridge and went inside, feeling the luxuriously cool air, hearing the comforting hum of the air conditioner. The saloon and galley of the *Sea Fever* were paneled in richly polished teak. Bone-white, tightly woven curtains could be drawn over the big windows along both sides. The furniture, which included a small but formal dining table and chairs, was also teak, the seating pieces upholstered in a Chinese pattern of blue and white linen. The thick, blue rug on the saloon floor was English and pure wool. Ira had picked out everything himself and after two years he still liked it. He wouldn't think of selling it, except that he had a problem: he was restless. At thirty-seven he had discovered there was nothing left that he wanted to do and hadn't already done.

In the galley he kicked off his deck shoes, put away the food, and took out Scotch and a can of plain soda. The sun was over the yardarm, and he was tired. He was adding ice to a glass when he sensed the tiny vibration that meant someone had stepped down onto his boat.

Physically, Ira was immediately ready to fight. Hair rose on the back of his neck, adrenaline pumped, tightening his muscles; his face hardened into a bronze mask. His breathing altered, became deeper, supplying extra oxygen. This was all automatic, for there's an old marine rule that no one comes aboard a boat without formal permission, a rule so well-known that when it's broken, it's almost always a thief. Someone, Ira thought, who'd seen him leave and hadn't seen him return. His bare feet made no sound as he crossed the saloon to the glass-topped door and eased aside the curtain.

The woman standing outside was very slim—though the loose, white suit she wore effectively disguised her exact shape—dark-haired and somehow expensive looking. Not a thief; just someone who either had the wrong boat or was ignorant of marine manners. Ira's adrenaline drained away. Pushing the door open, he stepped out to set her straight, perhaps help her find whatever she was looking for. He opened his mouth to speak to her, then she turned her head and immediately stiffened, staring at him like someone who has suddenly seen a wild animal and wonders if there is danger. Ira stared back, amazed by her reaction.

Diane Roberts knew she should speak, but couldn't. Her blue gaze took in his tousled, brown-gold hair and tiger eyes, slid jerkily over a carved, sensual mouth and down a tanned and blatantly male body, naked except for a pair of worn and clinging shorts. She recognized her own reaction at once, and her carefully honed defenses against his kind bristled. A stud, she thought, and then, seeing the sudden flare of interest in his sultry gaze, wondered if he had read her mind.

"I'm sorry," she said finally. "They told me at the office that this boat might be for sale, and there seemed to be no one around...."

What interested Ira was the fact that this woman was acutely uncomfortable. She wasn't exactly frightened, but wary. It was in the tremor of a muscle along her delicate jaw, in the flat tone of her voice. Hoping to reassure her, he spoke softly and casually looked away, breaking eye contact.

"I see. As a matter of fact, the boat may be for sale. Do you think you might be interested?"

Diane was rapidly regaining her poise. She told herself his sudden appearance had startled her. And she did like the boat. She looked away as he had. "I might be.

It's about the right size. How many will she accommodate?"

Ira smiled. "She sleeps six in three large staterooms. Normally a yacht this size sleeps eight, but she's custom-built and the cabins are larger than usual."

The blue eyes regarded him gravely, not dropping below his chin. "Is it best to build instead of buy?"

"It's one way to get exactly what you want. But it takes time." He wondered if he should add that it also took more money. Somehow he didn't think money was one of her problems. "I'll be happy to show you through," he added. "If nothing else, you might get an idea of what you'd want."

She started to refuse, then smiled, her eyes warming. "That's kind of you. I'd like to see it, if it's all right. You're the captain, then?"

"Yes. It's no trouble." He turned and opened the access door and ushered her in, realizing as she went past him that it was the only time she'd moved since he'd first seen her. She was graceful, making no unnecessary movements. He also noticed her perfume—a light scent of flowers and woman, and wondered why she hadn't done something about that little hump in her nose. Maybe, he thought, she was one of those who feared the knife.

Diane stopped in the corner of the saloon and swept the place with a slow glance, taking it all in. "Good," she said. "I like simple colors, simple design."

He was right behind her; she could hear him breathing, feel the light touch of his breath on her hair. She moved away a little. "That's a gas stove, isn't it? Is there a cook aboard?"

"No. I'm a fair cook myself."

Diane raised her brows. "Multi-talented? The owner has a bargain in you—captain and cook both." Idly drawing her fingers across the top of the dining table, she went through the galley, glanced at the half-open doorway into the forward wheelhouse, then started down the few steps of a companionway to a closed door. "I suppose this leads to the staterooms?"

Ira shut his open mouth. So, she thought he was just a hired captain. And now cook! That was what he got for wearing faded, ragged-out shorts. Resisting the impulse to tell her who owned, piloted, lived and cooked on this yacht, he said, "It does if you keep going forward. If you turn aft, you'll be in the engine room. Twin-turbo Cats, by the way."

"Cats?" Her hand on the door, she turned and looked up at him, her blue eyes questioning, wary again. He stared back at her, puzzled. How old was she? Twenty-eight, maybe more. Rich, fashionable, seemingly intelligent, yet so damn unsure of herself. He smiled, stepping down, reached past her and opened the door.

"The engines. Caterpillar diesels."

"Oh." She was through the door, face flushed, hands straightening the already straight edge of her jacket. "Now, let's see...."

Ira was considerate. He took over in a businesslike manner, throwing open the doors to the two smaller staterooms and their shower-equipped baths, neat, twin beds and built-in storage, then on to the luxurious master stateroom, with its mussed, king-size bed and mirrored walls, its black-tile Jacuzzi and sauna. The stereo was on, playing softly, and he turned it off, wishing he'd made the bed that morning. It all looked too lush, almost voluptuous, and he sensed her discomfort. But what the hell! He hadn't advertised an open house....

"Well, that's about it," he said briskly, shepherding her toward the steps, "unless you want to see the engines. Actually, if I—if the owner decides to sell and you decide you might like to buy, you should hire a marine surveyor. It's the only safe way to buy a used boat."

Diane murmured agreement. It was what she would have done anyway, but she didn't say so. She went rapidly through the galley and saloon and was opening the door to the outside deck when Ira spoke again.

"If you aren't in too much of a hurry," he said, wondering why he bothered, "stay and have a drink with me. I hate to drink alone."

Diane let out her breath. "Oh, I shouldn't . . . I need to check in. . . ." She stopped. Looking out, she saw that the sun had set, the evening breeze was rattling a loose sail someone hadn't tied properly. It was cooler, the air was fresher. Darkness was falling fast, but that didn't matter. There was no patient, old man waiting for her at home—no one at all. No one worrying. There was really no reason in the world why she couldn't stay for one drink. She turned back and found his warm gaze moving slowly over her face, touching the open neck of her blouse. Her lids shutting out her thoughts, she swung away.

"Very kind of you," she said. "But I'd better not."

2

IRA FOLLOWED DIANE onto the deck, grabbed a line and pulled the boat closer to the concrete wall of the slip. Helping her up, he wished her a good evening and still pushed by a whim he didn't analyze, added, "If you decide to take another look at the boat, call me. My name is Ira Nicholson."

She caught her breath and smiled. "Thank you. I'm Diane Roberts, and I'll be back to take another look."

Now that she was leaving, he wanted to ask when, he wanted to suggest tomorrow. He did neither, because she wasn't his type and he couldn't figure out why he would bother. Instead, he stepped up onto the concrete walkway beside her, his broad, bare shoulders shining in the glare of the dock light, his face in shadow. "I'll walk with you," he said, taking her arms. "With the office closed, the parking lot gets dark early."

Diane glanced up at him, conscious of his bare torso, aware of his warmth and his scent, salty and male. At her car Nicholson opened the door and stood back with a pleasant smile. "I enjoyed meeting you. Come around anytime."

As she drove away, Diane felt lonely and strange, knowing she was going home to an empty house. Six years ago, when she had moved in with Yuri, people had tramped in and out at all hours, family and friends. It had been wonderful to have a lively household after having no one but her complaining and reclusive father.

"Up to you," she whispered to herself on an indrawn breath. "You want lively, *you* make it lively." She saw her turn ahead and swerved, cutting in front of another car to get into the outside lane. There was room to spare, but the car's horn blared angrily, the driver shouting and shaking a fist. She ignored him, thinking hard, automatically heading for the causeway to the beach.

Now that she'd left the yacht and the man on it, Diane wished she had stayed for that drink. Certainly she wasn't living up to her promise to Yuri. Maybe it had been too long since she had done anything spontaneous; maybe she'd never learn how.

She could go back to living with her father. But she had lived with him after she had been to college, and it was like living with a cranky, possessive warden in a luxurious prison cell, with the rest of the world shut out and forgotten.

Get out, Yuri had said. Had he thought, or feared, that she'd hole up again in her father's house? *Go forth into the world. Find happiness. Adventure.*

Today she had met someone new for the first time in months. Ira Nicholson. She had felt adventurous, thinking of buying and sailing the *Sea Fever*. Crossing the crowded causeway toward the glittering explosion of lights on Miami Beach, she laughed, a quick little bubble of wry amusement. *Find a man to share with.* Share what? Certainly Yuri hadn't meant anything as blatantly sexy as that huge, tumbled bed. Yuri, bless him, had had an old man's sentiment, an old man's dream of poetic love.

She thought how strange it was, considering Yuri's sharp intelligence, that he had still believed in romantic love between a man and woman. He had sworn he and his first wife Trudy, who had died early, had loved like that. Diane's mouth twisted. Perhaps they had, but it could never happen to her. For her, what was called love could happen as well in a black-tile Jacuzzi as anywhere else, and last as long. Not that she'd tried it lately. Love had cost her the life of an unborn baby, leaving only scars. After that, it had been a relief to live with Yuri in a state of affectionate celibacy.

The traffic gradually eased as she left the causeway and turned into an area of fine houses on the west side of Miami Beach. Once away from the main avenues the streets were quiet, the estates large. After a few blocks she swung in toward a high, stone wall backed by arching trees, her headlights sweeping bronze gates, a plaque with the name Stephan. She touched a button in her car and the gates silently opened. She drove in, wincing as she heard them clang shut behind her.

THE SUN WAS JUST UP when Ira came yawning from the cabin to sit on his deck with a first cup of coffee. Big John Thomas was hosing off the concrete walkway a slip away. When he saw Ira, he came to sit on the edge of the walk. Tanned and muscular, wearing a neat, brown beard and cutoff jeans, he grinned and lighted a pipe.

"Well, is she going to buy?"

"Oh, so you sent the lady down?"

"Sure. Rose said you were thinking of selling, and you don't find that kind of money just layin' around anywhere. I figured you'd jump at the chance."

Ira shook his head. "I'm not even sure I want to sell. And she didn't ask the price. She can't be too serious."

"She don't have to ask. If she wants it, she'll buy it. You ever hear of Yuri Stephan?"

"Mr. Real Estate? Sure. I heard he died last week."

Big John laughed. "She was his, uh, partner, so they say. She got the business and his home, where she lived."

Brows raised, Ira gave him a cynical smile. "A bit young for him, but fell in love with his money?"

"I'd bet on it. Yuri died Wednesday morning, and she put his holdings up for sale Wednesday afternoon."

Ira swore softly. "Strange. I would have said she wasn't that kind. Shows what I know about women."

"I thought you knew all about women."

"Like the guy in the art gallery—I know nothing about the subject, I just know what I like. I liked her, but I'll keep my defenses up if she comes around." Ira laughed suddenly. "Not that she'll come on to me. For one thing, she thinks I'm a hired captain on the *Sea Fever*."

"You're safe," Big John agreed, laughing. "Enjoy it."

IRA NICHOLSON spent the rest of the morning in the heart of the business section in old Miami. He made several stops, the last one at a branch office of the Stephan Real Estate company, where he knew the manager. He worked the conversation around to Yuri Stephan's death, which wasn't hard, since Tom Russell, the manager, was nervous about the coming sale. Tom brought up Diane's name, wishing she would hang on to the business instead of selling.

Ira leaned back, steepled his long fingers thoughtfully and asked why. "Usually," he added, "what a woman does is bring in some so-called expert to run the company, and half the time the expert steals her blind and the value drops. Better for all of you if she sells while it's healthy."

"Not in this case," Russell said gloomily. "Diane's been running the whole shebang for four years. She's damn good, too. But I guess she's tired of it." He looked at Ira and smirked. "She earned that money. Six years with an old man is a long time when you're young and good-looking."

"I've seen her," Ira said. "And I'd bet she didn't spend all of her leisure time with old Yuri Stephan." His jaw snapped shut in surprise. As a matter of personal pride, he never made suggestive remarks about another couple's love life, no matter how obviously mismatched they were. He got up, ready to leave before he said something stupid again.

"You'd lose," Russell said mildly. "When he got old, Yuri did most of his business at home, which meant we were all in and out of there at any hour of the night or day. Diane was always at the main office or with Yuri. For one thing, she didn't trust anyone else to make sure he took his pills."

"Pills?"

"Yep. Yuri had a bad heart condition when he took her on. He was seventy-two then and careless with his pills. His doctor said Diane was the medicine that kept him alive for another six years."

Ira was more confused than ever when he left. Angry at himself for hunting down gossip about a woman he barely knew, he decided to forget Diane Roberts and find someone to have a little fun with. He went into a bar, ordered a drink and carried it to a telephone, sipping as he looked up a number. Suzy. Suzy would be home, probably in bed, since it wasn't noon yet. He waited, listening to the distant ring.

"Hello?" Sleepy, sweet, the voice broke in. "Hello?"

Ira gently replaced the receiver. He might want to sell the boat, after all. Suppose the Roberts woman came by today and found him entertaining Suzy. She'd probably stick that silly, crooked nose into the air and stalk away.

And he'd lose a sale. He put the half-full glass onto the bar and left, walking down the street to his car, fully aware he was making up excuses. He simply wanted to be there, alone, if Diane Roberts came.

DIANE CLIMBED OUT of the swimming pool to take a call, throwing on a terry robe over her black bikini, wiping her wet hands before she handled the phone.

"Where were you yesterday afternoon, Diane? I expected you here by two o'clock, at the latest. You know how I worry, when I expect you and you don't show up."

Diane counted to ten. Her father's petulant, sagging face was as clear to her as if he were present, and so were all the miserable years she had spent, trying to please him. *My curse*, she thought, *is an excellent memory.* She forced a pleasant tone. "Sorry. I thought I told you I'd be tied up all day."

"You did," Harrington Roberts said morosely, "and you lied. I called Henry Wilton at noon, and he said you'd left an hour before. Naturally, I thought you'd come here. This is your home now, my dear. Cora has spent two days airing and getting your suite ready for you. When are you selling that house?"

Temper flashed a brilliant red mist in front of Diane's eyes. Over and over she'd told her father she wasn't going home. He'd just made up his mind not to accept her decision. She waited a moment for the worst of her anger to pass and then spoke. "Never," she said unevenly, and paused again to control her voice. "I'm keeping it, Father. I'm going to live in it when I settle down. If you want family around you, I suggest you marry Cora."

"What? What are you saying? Do you expect me to marry a servant? Cora's the housekeeper!"

Diane gritted her teeth. "That isn't all she is, though, is it? After twenty years of warming your bed, Cora needs a little security. If you had a shred of decency..." She sighed and stopped talking to the dead line. Handing the telephone back to the maid, whose face was frozen with the effort of appearing deaf, she slipped on her clogs and headed across the patio to her room. "I'm going shopping. If my father calls again, you don't know when I'll be back." She paused at the door. "You won't be lying. Tell Agnes I won't be here for dinner." She left, wrestling with the remnants of fury. Wrapped in the protective cocoon of Yuri's affection, she had forgotten just how impossible Harrington Roberts could be. And how lonely life could be. Standing in her shower, she told herself it was time to act. Time to fling herself into life. Climbing out, reaching for a towel, she laughed breathlessly. *Take the chance, then.* Maybe Ira Nicholson would catch her.

THE DOCK LIGHTS at Biscay Yacht Basin were blinking on, one here and one there, sometimes several at once in the growing twilight. It had rained earlier and the air was cooler, the concrete walkways wet and dark, the decks of the boats beaded with drops of water. Ira sat on the aft deck of the *Sea Fever* wearing white duck trousers and a loose gold and white striped cotton shirt that made his shoulders and chest look as wide as a wall. He had dropped into a canvas lounge chair, his long legs sprawled, hands loosely clasped around a highball glass and head bent, brooding over melting ice cubes.

"Good evening."

His head shot up, his eyes zeroed in on a slim wraith in floating, gossamer draperies, standing on the walkway. He put the glass down on the deck and stood up, swallowing. Diane Roberts was full of surprises.

"I didn't think you were coming."

She laughed softly, the sound murmurous and sweet. "I wasn't sure myself. But here I am. I thought perhaps we could have dinner and talk about the boat."

"Great!" He plunged across the deck, awkwardly kicking the glass, which skidded through a scupper and disappeared with a small splash. "Let me help you aboard." He pulled the boat closer and reached, his hands grasping her narrow waist and swinging her down. Under the layers of thin chiffon her smooth muscles moved warmly against his palms; her scent was faint, but tantalizing.

Ira stepped away to look her over with what he tried to make a confident smile. He needed a minute or so to get a new start here, before he fell over his own feet. Not only had she surprised the hell out of him by even showing up, she looked fantastic. The top of her dress was sleeveless, the wide neckline scooped low and loose around the swell of small breasts, while the layers of misty chiffon drifted down in veils of handkerchief points circling round, tight hips. The soft movement of the silk was constant, lifting and billowing, fluttering down. The skirt was the same, layers on layers, all soft motion in the light breeze, points dancing around her slender legs. Reaching out, Ira caught a fluttering edge in midair and let the silk slide sinuously between his fingers.

"Lovely. You should have warned me that you would be disguised as Queen Titania. Should I worry about spells?"

"She lent me her faery gown," Diane answered solemnly, "but not her magic. May I have a drink?"

His surprise kept growing. How could she change so much? She was warm, flirtatious. He laughed, feeling a shock of pure pleasure, and took her arm, sweeping her toward the door to the saloon.

"Anything you want. If I don't have it, I'll get it."

They talked, leaning toward each other, Diane on the couch, Ira in a chair, their knees touching. Mostly they ignored their drinks.

"Has the owner decided on a price?"

"Not yet. But I've been thinking, if you buy, you'll need a crew. You'll need a licensed captain."

"What should I do, go to an agency or advertise for one?"

"Hire me."

Diane smiled. "I'd like that. But something tells me you wouldn't stay long." She watched him jump up and get a tray, a couple of wooden dishes, which he filled with chips and dip.

"Try these. And then we've got to find dinner. You need to eat. You're thin. You've got bones like a sparrow." His gold-brown eyes brooded over the soft, tender hollows above her fragile collarbones, then widened when she laughed.

"How flattering, Ira. Sparrow bones!"

The brooding look cleared and he laughed with her. "You must know you're a pound or two short of perfection."

Diane had begun on the dip, munching as she dipped another chip and offered it to him. When he refused, she ate it and reached for another. "The saying is," she reminded him, "that no one is ever thin enough or rich enough."

"Mmm-hmm. And you're the exception that proves the rule?"

She frowned, but kept on eating. "I hope you're going to be an exception to the usual men I meet. I hate having my personal worth equated with my financial assets." She raised her eyes to his. "In this morning's mail I received five sympathy notes on the loss of my partner and six proposals of marriage. From strangers! I feel like a lottery prize."

Ira grinned. "If you were, I'd buy tickets. But marriage? No way. I'm terrified by the mere idea."

She leaned back and laughed. "Wonderful! So am I. Are there more of those chips?"

"More?" He looked at the bowl, which was empty, and shook his head. "You are hungry."

"Yes. Yes, I am." She sat still, looking at him with a faint smile. "What are you going to do about it?"

He studied her smile, the warmth in her blue eyes, the barest hint of a quiver in her full, lower lip. Then he stood up and reached for her hand. "For starters, I'm walking you over to the Neptune Café for a steak and a lobster tail. Come along, Sparrow."

The Neptune Café was an old, wooden building among a bunch of empty, vandalized warehouses left over from better days. Outside, the Neptune looked as if it could use a coat of paint and a timber or two to brace the sagging roof, but inside everything from the plank floor to the raftered ceiling was shining clean, and the odors of steak and seafood were appetizing.

Small, intimate booths lined the walls. There was a jukebox, shimmering with color, bouncing with rock and roll. The waitresses bounced with it, wearing skirts and blouses and bobby socks. Diane stared, fascinated.

"Everything has a theme these days," Ira said, seating her in a booth. "They say the Neptune opened in the fifties. One of the things they serve is nostalgia." He slid in beside her, crowding her a little, unable to resist the lure of her slender body touching his. She looked up at him, her face shadowed, her eyes and parted lips catching a gleam of golden light from the shaded lamp. Ira felt his pulse jump. Her closeness, her scent, the soft, parted lips were too much. He bent, enclosing her mouth with his, his tongue luxuriously following the soft, wet velvet edges, sucking in her lower lip to bite gently. She drew in her breath with a soundless gasp and touched his roving tongue with the curling tip of hers.

"Well, what'll you two lovebirds have this evening?"

Breaking away, Ira stared blankly at the waitress who had somehow materialized at their booth. "Surf and turf," he managed, "green salad, light dressing. Coffee later."

Writing, the waitress smiled at Diane. "You?"

"The same. Medium rare on the steak."

"That's the same, too," the waitress said pertly and winked at Ira. "Your boyfriend here eats medium-rare steak eight days out of the week." She flounced off, her dirndl skirt swinging. Ira reached for Diane's hand and held it, under the table.

"I'm sorry if I embarrassed you."

Shaken and too warm, Diane shook her head. "You didn't. Anyway, I cooperated."

"Beautifully," Ira said huskily. "I hope you plan to continue. Do you?"

"I can't answer that. I don't know." She laughed and took her hand from his, afraid he'd feel her pounding pulse. "I haven't been making any plans, Ira. Just . . . letting things happen, I guess." She leaned back, trying for composure. "Maybe it's wrong, but I'm tired of living on a schedule. Can you believe that I don't want to know what I'll be doing and where I'm going to be to-morrow?"

"Yes, easily," Ira answered and relaxed beside her, looping an arm around her shoulders. "You've just described my usual life-style."

"Really?"

"Really." Stroking her hair with his free hand, he eased her head onto his shoulder. "I'm an absolute expert at living by impulse. If you'd like to try it for a while, you couldn't find a better teacher. What do you say?"

His shoulder was solid and warm, his side against her taut and hard, his scent a wonderful mixture of soap and musky maleness. Her upward glance caught the slow darkening of his gold-brown eyes. She turned her head, fighting a losing battle with her excellent memory. It had been years since a young man had been this close to her, but she hadn't forgotten a damn thing.

"Ira..." She sat up, freeing herself from his arm. "Let's keep it cool. We've just met." He was still relaxed, lounging on the padded back of the bench, grinning, his golden gaze warming her skin where it touched.

"You're right," he said, "but I'm looking forward to getting to know you very well."

His meaning was clear in his eyes, in his slow, sensual smile. Her pulse fluttered erratically. A strong flare of heat burned inside. He definitely attracted her, and she had to start somewhere. But...why start with a man like him? Practiced, charming—probably used to playing the squire to female guests on that yacht. Maybe waiting for a woman like her—single, lonely and rich enough to give him the easy life he wanted. She'd had one of those, and one was enough.

"That's flattering, Ira." She gave him a cocky grin. "And tempting. But it would take a great deal of thought."

Ira had rarely been brushed off or met with this much resistance from a woman. But there had been times, and he'd worked out a way to deal with it. First he was courteous and understanding. Second he was gone. He had always felt there were too many lovely women in the world to argue with one who wanted to think. But this time he surprised himself.

"All right, Sparrow. You think and I'll wait. The offer still holds."

3

"THE DINNER was delicious, and I loved the place," Diane said and stumbled slightly. They were walking along the street of tumbledown warehouses with nothing to guide them but the light of a pale, half moon. She clung to his arm, a high heel slipping in the rubble. "Sorry to be so awkward. If I come this way again I'll wear hiking boots."

In answer Ira swept her into his arms and walked on, laughing softly as she clutched his shoulder and protested in a startled squeak.

"Shh. You'll wake the drunks and druggies who sleep in these buildings." She was quiet, turning her head to look, her hair touching his cheek in a fragrant cloud. Lord, but she was light. Light and soft, the skin of the arm around his neck like warm silk, the small, firm pillow of her breast pressing against his chest.

"You can put me down," she whispered into his ear. "I won't make any noise. I didn't know before."

"I like this better."

She was silent, staring at his dark, strong-featured face. He was breathing easily, walking with a spring in his step, carrying her as if she weighed no more than a child. Even so, she tightened her hold on his shoulders to help support her weight, and saw the corner of his mouth turn up.

"Afraid you're too heavy for me?"

"No." She looked ahead, seeing they were nearly at the docks and the glaring, yellow lights. "But we're past the worst of it. Let me down before the dock master sees us."

Ira stopped, letting her slide down his body, wrapping his arms around her, burying a hand in her thick hair. Diane could feel his heat through the gossamer layers of her dress, and caught the clean musk of his scent as he leaned down and kissed her. As his tongue slid between her lips, her whole body reacted in a wild rush of desire. She burned for more, her tongue tangling with his, her small breasts tightening, pushing against his chest, her hips tilting, moving hungrily against his instantaneous arousal. Ira gasped, lowering his hands to her buttocks to drag her closer, tighter, and in the same instant Diane jerked away with a stifled sound and turned her back to him.

"Damn," she whispered. "Damn, damn, damn! I'm sorry, Ira. That was...stupid of me." She bent her head, scrubbing at her cheeks with both hands, pushing back her hair, finally turning toward him again. Light glinted across her face. Pale, half-angry, she was wholly embarrassed. He reached for her and she stepped back, shaking her head.

"I didn't mean any of that—that come-on. And I'm truly sorry."

Ira was silent. She had meant it. Or at least her body had. But her anger at herself was real. She was honestly upset, not playing games.

Tentatively he reached again, but this time only for her hand. "It's all right, Sparrow. Let's walk."

She took his hand and went with him, but only as far as the marina office and her car. There she stopped and looked up at him, calm and reserved again. "It's been a very nice evening, Ira. However, I think I'd better go home."

He wasn't surprised. He had figured she wouldn't want the intimacy of the boat after that kiss. Something, he couldn't know what, had torn her up. He let go of her hand and stood beside her, his eyes on the myriad of colored lights across the dark bay, and told himself to get the hell out of this. He didn't need problems. And anyway, she wasn't his kind, not by a long shot. *Tell her goodbye. Tell her you're leaving in the morning for a long cruise.* He shifted from one foot to the other and looked down at her.

"What do you want to do tomorrow?"

She blinked. "I'm supposed to see the president of the board at the Stephan Corporation," she said. "He believes there's a winner in the buy bids and wants to talk it over. Later I'm having Yuri's daughter and son to dinner." She paused, staring at him thoughtfully. "Paul and Anna are older and not much fun, but I'd like to have you, too. Except you might be terribly bored...."

"Just tell me where you live."

She laughed a little and let go of his hand to search out a card in her purse. "Here's the address, Ira. Blow your horn at the gate and someone will let you in. I appreciate this a lot. I need an impartial guest around to keep things on an even keel. Dinner's at eight, so be there by seven, and don't bother to dress." She went to her car in a flutter of pale chiffon, a tapping of heels, a quick wave.

Ira watched her zoom out and shrugged, slipping the card into his shirt pocket. An impartial guest? He couldn't know what she meant by that, but perhaps it would be interesting. So much for cutting himself loose from trouble and saying goodbye.

DIANE MET with Henry Wilton and the rest of the directors at ten o'clock the next morning. This time she came in through the main entrance, stopping to speak to every employee she met, beginning with the security guard. She was feeling a bit nostalgic, worrying about someone else taking over Yuri's company, yet knowing this was what he had wanted for her.

Henry greeted her at the entrance to the directors' meeting room. He looked pleased with himself.

"We've managed to keep this under wraps," he said, escorting her into the hushed formality of the thickly carpeted, beautifully furnished room. "These men don't want publicity until the contract is signed." Seating her in his usual place at the head of the large, oval table, he sat down with her to wait for the others. "You're looking wonderful, Diane. Leisure agrees with you. Have you seen Paul lately?"

Always alert to changes in a tone of voice, Diane glanced quickly at Henry. With no real authority in the business, Paul still was a Stephan, the son of Yuri's second wife. He used his position as a family member to harry and criticize the executives in the corporation, and from the sound of Henry's voice he had been the latest victim. "No," she said, "but I will tonight. What's on your mind?"

"Paul told me today he was thinking of making a bid for the business."

Diane stared, then laughed. "He was trying to get your goat, Henry. He knows absolutely nothing about business. I don't think he could run a newsstand."

"I think he meant it."

"You're serious?" At Henry's nod Diane looked thoughtful. She never discounted Henry's judgment, though his statement was hard to believe. "All right. But he won't be a problem if we accept this other bid. I'll tell him tonight that the Stephan Corporation is sold."

"That's fine! He'll take it from you. Uh-oh, here they come...." Henry was on his feet, smiling, his hand out in greeting as men filed in the open door.

Watching, Diane felt her eyes widen and a surprised smile play over her lips. Three of the four men who accompanied the directors, Murray, Hill, and Black, were known to her. The fourth, Stanton Rogers, she recognized from newspaper pictures. Four of the giants in subdivision and mall development in Florida; four men who really knew the scope of Yuri Stephan's holdings, who would see to it that the corporation prospered. She felt a moment of intense regret that Yuri couldn't see this, then settled back. When this was over she'd be free.

PRECISELY AT SEVEN, Ira pulled up in his rental car and stopped at the address Diane had given him. He stared at the high walls, the heavy, fancily wrought bronze gates and the long, twilight vista of manicured landscape. Financially he'd come a long way from his beginnings, though not this far. But what difference did it make? He wasn't going to marry the woman. He blew the horn and the gates swung open majestically. Driving in, watching in the rearview mirror as they closed, he considered what a handsome cage they made for his Sparrow.

Yuri Stephan's mansion had been built in the twenties, with a red, barrel tile roof, three stories, beautiful, Spanish windows with arches and intricate, black iron guards, creamy stucco walls and long, colonnaded and arched loggias. The loggias led off in every direction, red tile roofs snaking through the shrubbery, using the excuse of a summerhouse, a pool, a guest house as destinations. The place was in perfect shape, not a fault to mar its beauty. It could have been built yesterday, yet Ira would have taken odds that it had been here long before Yuri left Russia.

He parked and strode briskly along the brick walk to the narrow verandah that ran across the front of the house.

Someone, he thought, mounting the wide steps, had been watching for arrivals. The door was easing open, pushed by a hand and arm in a black sleeve, and then Diane slipped past the man standing there and put a slim hand on Ira's arm.

"I wasn't at all sure you'd come, but I knew if you did, you'd be on time. Paul and Anna never are." She turned to the other man. "Direct the others to the terrace, please, Norman."

She took Ira through an astonishing foyer, crowded with antique furniture, the floor covered by old, Turkish carpets, down a long, paneled hall, and out again onto a brick terrace, dotted with huge pots of rose-bushes trained into small trees. There she let go of his arm and whirled away, stretching herself in the cool, fresh air, slim arms high, rising onto her toes. She was wearing white again, like the day he met her, only tonight it was a billowy, full skirt and a camisole top with lace and silver-ribbon straps. She looked young and earnest as she breathed in the deep, slow, yoga way, and then relaxed into a normal pose. She looked at Ira's bemused expression and laughed. "You think I'm crazy, I know. But I'm trying to let go of tension. These evenings with Paul . . . they always seem interminable. You were good to come."

"It's my pleasure," Ira said formally, thrusting his hands into his pants pockets to keep from reaching for her. "Want to give me a few pointers on the other guests?"

"Mmm, good idea. First, a drink." She took his arm again, steering him toward the bar. "If you'll do the honors, Ira." She watched him move behind the bar, as relaxed in this setting as he was on the yacht.

Pouring, adding ice and soda, Ira felt that Diane was bracing herself for something unpleasant. He couldn't imagine why she would worry. She'd done all right on her own, capturing Yuri Stephan. How many worries could she have? Yet he felt protective. He supposed it was because she looked so impossibly fragile with her fine bones, her small hands, the narrow, blue-veined wrists. He followed her to a table, bringing the drinks.

"Now tell me," he said when they were seated, "what hold this Paul has over you."

"Why, none," Diane answered. "But he's Yuri's son."

"Did Yuri allow Paul to bother him?"

Diane stared at him thoughtfully. "No, he didn't. When Paul became argumentative, Yuri sent him out of the room. Are you suggesting I might do the same?"

"It's your house, isn't it?"

She laughed in that soft, murmurous way he liked. "Yes, of course. I suppose I could try. But—well, Paul is easily hurt, and that upsets Anna. I really love Anna."

"Anna is Paul's sister?"

"Stepsister. Anna is the daughter of Yuri's first wife. Paul is the son of his second wife. But Anna, who is ten years older than Paul, is very maternal toward him."

Ira leaned back and grinned. "And you tread a careful line between them. Your life with a fabulously rich man wasn't all glorious fun, was it?"

Diane frowned, looking away. "My years with Yuri were the happiest of my life. He was the best friend I ever had."

"That's quite an accolade," Ira said quietly. "I'm sorry. What I said was stupid." It was stupid. Why was he reacting aggressively toward an old man—a dead man? For that matter, he ought to quit trying to protect Diane Roberts. He knew what she was.

She smiled and made a small gesture, dismissing the subject, and looked toward the house. "I believe I hear Anna and Lon."

Ira turned and rose politely. They were all there, he saw. Anna, a tall, deep-bosomed, gentle-faced woman of fifty-odd, wearing a blue and white, silk print; Lon Brodorski, a large, heavyset man wearing slacks, a casual jacket and an amiable expression; and hidden behind them a small, pale man in a gray suit, who frowned and pursed his lips when he saw Ira. Paul, no doubt.

In the natural order of things, Diane presented Ira to Paul last. After a bare semblance of a handshake, Paul ignored him, turning to Diane. "I thought this gathering would be a conference, Diane, not a social occasion. Surely, if you are actually going to sell the Stephan Corporation—which, I must say, is terribly unwise—you need advice from all of us."

Diane smiled. "This gathering is more in the nature of a small celebration, Paul. What kind of a cocktail would you like to have, Anna? I see Alycides mixing Manhattans."

Lon had already moved in on Ira; they were talking and drifting away to the bar, where an elderly Mexican had arrived and taken over. Paul turned and looked. "It seems rather bad taste," he said before Anna could answer, "to invite a young man as your dinner partner, so soon after Father's death. He's probably another fortune hunter, like the last one you had. I thought you'd learned—"

"Paul," Anna interrupted firmly, "shut up. I'll have a Manhattan, Diane, and I think your young man is very attractive. I am sure Father would have approved."

Diane gave her a grateful look. "Thanks, Anna. I happen to know he would." She left to fetch a tray of drinks.

Obviously wounded, Paul maintained a dignified silence through the rest of the predinner conversations, but Diane expected an argument later. She said so in a whisper to Ira. Standing with her at the edge of the terrace, he grinned at her lazily, his teeth very white in the growing darkness.

"Say the word, and I'll put him out by the scruff of his neck."

Diane was shocked but amused. "Please don't! He's harmless, really. He only wants to feel important."

She was looking up at him, her eyes glinting a dark blue, her mouth curved in a half smile. He touched her hair, pretending to stroke back a blowing strand, and left his hand on the nape of her slender neck, his thumb caressing the soft skin beneath the fall of hair. He had judged Paul Stephan in the first few minutes as a weak little martinet, and his usually slow anger had stirred and wakened when he overheard Paul's remark about a fortune hunter. He would have enjoyed escorting him to a door then and kicking him out. Not because he was harmful, only because he was rude.

"There have been troublemakers before," he said, after a moment, "who only wanted to feel important. Napoleon, for instance. Adolf Hitler. Alexander the Great."

Diane burst into laughter and took his arm. "Come on, I know Lon is starving. Let's lead them in. Besides..." She turned with him and started for the house. "I never thought of Alexander the Great as a troublemaker."

"All those people he conquered thought he was."

She was laughing again as they headed for the dining room. Behind them, Ira heard Paul complaining again to Anna.

"Having everything her own way is making her as silly as a schoolgirl. How could she make a sensible decision without advice?"

The dining room was no more in keeping with the open, airy style of the house than the foyer had been. Antiques, mostly heavy, carved pieces from eastern European countries, crowded the large space. Paintings in dark, rich colors almost covered the walls, a collection of massive, highly ornate, silver bowls and platters glittered on the tops of chests and buffet. A crystal chandelier spread dazzling light on the table, set with more silver, fine china and crystal.

Seated at Diane's right, eating duck *à l'orange* and drinking a very nice champagne, Ira tried to sort out the stream of impressions assaulting him from all sides. He took in the ornate furnishings, the lack of style, and dismissed them. He had never been interested in things, only people. He had liked Lon Brodorski on sight, a great, friendly bear of a man with an unexpectedly keen sense of humor. And Anna. Anna had defended Diane from Paul's waspish attack. As for Diane, Ira watched her with a wry admiration as she passed off caustic comments and rude questions from Paul with a pleasant smile, and, without being obvious, turned the subject to Lon and Anna's two sons, Lon, Jr. and Yuri II.

During Anna's proud monologue about her sons' latest exploits, Diane touched Ira's hand beneath the table.

"Like it?" she asked under her breath, and watched his slow grin. He answered her so quietly that his deep voice was more vibration than sound. But she heard him.

"The duck? Delicious. The champagne? Extraordinary." *The woman? Marvelously sexy.* He saw her look away, and wondered if she had seen the unspoken thought in his eyes.

"Heavens, Anna," Paul said peevishly, "that's really enough about your children, though I'm sure we're all pleased that they're doing well. Tell me, have either of them ever thought of going into the corporation?"

"Now, why would they want to do that? Lon is a lawyer, and Yuri has his medical degree. He'll be interning at Jackson Memorial."

"I simply asked—" Paul bristled "—don't make such a to-do of it. I'd like to point out that Diane is threatening to sell Father's lifework without even considering the rest of us."

Lon spoke up, his broad face puzzled. "Why shouldn't she, Paul? Your father signed over the corporation to her a year ago. You have your inheritance, more than you'll ever need, and you'll want her advice on managing it."

"I don't need advice," Paul said. "But she does." He looked furious, his face a dull red. "You should have consulted me, Diane. You know the corporation should be mine. I'm sure you influenced Father to give it to you, and I'll take you to court unless you include me in any further talks."

"There'll be no further talks," Diane said stiffly. "I signed a sales contract today. That's what I meant to tell you tonight." She was white, her eyes a burning blue, her curved lips now a straight line. "I had hoped you'd be glad for me. Finish your dinner and go, Paul. I'm tired of being insulted in my own house."

"What? What? You can't have sold this soon! I'll sue, damn you. I'll get an injunction. What right have you to tell me to get out of the house I was raised in? My *fa-*

ther's house." Paul's face was twisted with fury. "That's another thing you stole from me."

Ira stood, wondering just how impartial Diane wanted him to be. His hands itched to grab Paul Stephan's shirt and drag him across the table. "That's enough, Stephan," he started, and beside him Diane got up.

"Lon," she said, her voice shaky, "and Anna. I'm truly sorry this happened. Please finish your dinners and take Paul with you when you go. I'm leaving now with Mr. Nicholson and I don't know when I'll be back."

4

OUTSIDE, light blazed from the windows of the great house, glowed golden from the low-lit garden paths and winding loggias, and leaped upward into the underside of the old oak trees. Gleaming on the crooked and gnarled branches, it made the trees look even more enormous, magically growing higher, towering away into the dark sky. Diane fled beneath the twisted canopy, walking rapidly toward Ira's car. He followed silently, aware of her thrumming tension.

Leaving the grounds, the car tripped a signal to the gates and they swung open, offering freedom. Diane glanced back. From here the house was invisible, but the glow of its lights could be seen through the tops of the trees. Offering security? So did a jail, she thought. Breathing deeply, letting her shoulders drop, she caught Ira's glance.

"Thank you for bringing me out. I hope you didn't mind."

He smiled, the greenish light from the dash accentuating the deep clefts that appeared in his flat cheeks. "I didn't mind."

She had grabbed a handbag from the foyer table as they left, and now she stuffed it into the dash compartment and leaned back, looking ahead with furrowed brows.

"Anna will blame me for that scene. I'll end up losing her, I'm afraid. She's blind where Paul is concerned."

"Her husband isn't."

"Lon?" Diane turned her head to look at him. "I suppose you're right—he sees Paul clearly. But I'll lose him, too. He doesn't like having his Anna upset."

"Maybe, but I'd be willing to bet you won't lose any of them. Have you family of your own?"

"Only my father." She lowered the window and let the breeze blow onto her face and lift her thick hair from her neck. After a moment she added, "Even Paul is better company than Harrington Roberts."

Jolted, Ira stared at her. "The recluse? The man nobody knows?"

"I know him," Diane said, still looking out of the window. "They aren't missing a thing." She swung around and faced him, her eyes pained but mocking. "See what you've got yourself into, Ira? A bunch of crazy people."

"No," Ira returned, "not you. You're not crazy, Diane." *He* was, for thinking Harrington Roberts's daughter had taken up with an old man for money. "Neither are they," he went on, swallowing his shock. "They just want to keep you working. When we first talked, Lon said that now that Yuri is gone, you're their touchstone. Their good-luck piece."

Diane shook her head. "Lon was exaggerating. I've done nothing for them."

Ira laughed without humor. "From what he said, the three of them have kicked back and let the money roll in for years, while first their father and then you took care of all their investments. Who will do it now, if you don't?"

She was motionless, thinking, then faced forward again and relaxed. "They can hire someone. There are lots of good financial advisers. It's not going to be me. I'm not just trying to get out, Ira. I am out, as of today.

Whether Paul knows it or not, the corporation is gone. And in a week or less I'll be gone."

"Where?"

She laughed and stretched, straightening her slender legs, slumping bonelessly into the soft seat and twining her arms above her head. All at once she looked young and careless. "Who knows? First I have to find out if I have a yacht. Have you talked to the owner? Will he sell?"

"I haven't talked to anyone yet." Well, that much was true. Ira wished now he'd never let her think the *Sea Fever* belonged to someone else. He'd gotten over the thought of selling fast, but if he told her so, he might never see her again. "Listen," he added, struck by inspiration, "why not try her out? See if you like her? As long as you're getting out, you may as well get far enough out that they can't find you."

They were moving onto the mainland in heavy traffic, and Ira's eyes were glued to the jockeying cars. It gave Diane a chance to study him, and she took full advantage, her eyes scanning him slowly, searching out the tiny marks of habit or temper or laughter that helped one to judge a man.

Tonight, she thought, she had learned his protective instinct was strong, and he seemed able to control his temper. She discounted the frown grooves between his thick brows, because a man who went to sea would naturally have them. Grooves there, crinkles at the outer corners of the eyes. She approved of the corners of his broad mouth, which tilted upward. She studied his lips, firm but sensual. Sexy, like his eyes. Another strong instinct? She thought of his kiss and his hard body against hers and the memory became heat, spiraling hotly through her belly. Catching her breath, she tore her attention away and sat up, warm and slightly dizzy.

"Well," Ira said, still not looking at her, "will I do?"

There was a long silence while she struggled with old anxieties, fears and even embarrassment. But if she were ever going to try out Yuri's advice, she had to start somewhere.

"To be honest," she said, "I think you're extremely attractive. The problem is me. I'm not sure I'll ever make it with a man. I'm not even sure I want to try."

Ira glanced at her, startled. He had only meant to kid her for staring at him so long; but the question, coming on top of the invitation to go cruising, had evidently carried a meaning much more personal to her. Amazed, he reached over and took her hand, holding it and feeling the slight tremble in her fingers. *Watch it*, he told himself. *A rich man's daughter can be trouble on wheels.* Any woman that wealthy would be damn hard to handle.

"I'll chance it, love," he said, and drove on.

IRA HAD PLANNED to sit out on the *Sea Fever*'s deck with Diane, drinking brandy, talking about the cruise, watching the stars wheeling across the dark sky. But coming out the long dock, he saw it wouldn't work. A boisterous party was going on a couple of boats away from his, and there was no hope of getting it toned down by a complaint to the management—both Rose and Big John Thomas were among the guests. They hailed him as he passed and yelled an invitation, but he kept walking, his hand firm under Diane's arm.

"Thanks," he called back, "some other time. Have fun."

Aboard the *Sea Fever*, they went into the saloon and thankfully closed the door on the raucous noise.

"Brandy?"

"A little," Diane said, and followed him to the liquor cabinet, leaning on a counter and watching him pour.

"Where would we go on a cruise, Ira?"

He smiled and handed her a glass, his eyes in the shaded light glinting the same dark gold as the brandy. "Anywhere you like, from the Bahamas to the Keys. Or down to the Virgins, which would keep you out of Miami for quite a while."

She smiled, her face softened by dreams. "Could we really go that far? What's it like down there?"

"It depends on who you're with," he answered, and put a casual arm around her waist to lead her to the couch. "For instance," he went on, sitting down with her, "if you take some idiot who only wants glamour and luxury..."

"Hah!"

"What?"

"I said 'hah!' which is an expression conveying scorn," Diane said, leaning into the corner of the couch, trying not to laugh. "Where do you get off, pretending to be better than those glamour seekers? This isn't exactly a bargain-basement boat. Maybe it isn't yours, but you enjoy it."

Ira grinned. "True." Sitting on the edge of the couch, elbows on his knees, and holding the brandy snifter between his palms, he turned to study her. Her windblown, dark hair was a springing tangle around her slim neck, the lace and ribbon straps of her camisole top accented the fragility of those collarbones that made him call her Sparrow. But under the thin cotton of the camisole were the enticing points of small breasts that looked perfectly round in shape, perfectly sized to fit his palms. His gaze rose slowly from her breasts to her face. She had lost her teasing smile. Her blue eyes, meeting his, were warm and dark and questioning, her lips soft and parted.

Carefully Ira put his glass on the table and reached for hers. She handed it to him silently, and when he had put it down and turned back, her arms came up to hold him.

It was as she had sometimes dreamed it could be. He was passionate but gentle, and everything about him seemed right. His scent, the feel of his flesh, the way his mouth moved on hers, nudging her lips apart. Trembling, she licked the hot tip of his questing tongue and shuddered with pleasure when he thrust it inside her mouth.

His hands moved over her, their warmth and hunger felt through the thin cotton, and where they touched, the tight, frightened muscles relaxed and grew warm and hungry like the hands. She returned his caresses as well as she could, held down like that, pushed into the corner. She stroked his back, reaching up under his shirt to his smooth skin and the thick, ropelike muscles. Fascinated by the hard swell of arousal that touched her thighs, she reached down and stroked him there. Then slowly she became conscious of a change in him, an urgency; harsh, altered breathing. He was crowding her hard now into the corner of the couch, crushing her down, and then suddenly he jerked away, moving to a point where they didn't touch and leaning back, eyes closed, panting.

"I was losing control." He sounded chagrined. Opening his eyes, he looked at her with a faint smile. "I don't usually do that. I think I can promise that it won't happen again."

She nodded, acknowledging what he said without really taking it in. She sat up, smoothing her wrinkled dress. "It's all right, Ira. Actually, I . . . it was my fault."

Fault? He stared at her. She had been driving him crazy with those questing hands, but he sure as hell hadn't been objecting. He cleared his throat. "No. It's just the wrong place." He stood up and reached for her hand. "Let's find the right place."

Her eyes met his apologetically. "I'm sorry, but no. I'm beginning to think there isn't a right place for me. How about taking me home?"

Ira hesitated. Then, dropping his wide shoulders in a gesture of defeat, he laughed and sat down again. "All right. But will you promise me that if your family is still there, I get to throw Paul out for you?"

She smiled, touching his hand tentatively, curling her fingers loosely around his. "That's a limited yes—I'm sure they'll be gone. Now will you do something else for me? Ask the man who owns this pleasure palace if I can lease it for a month. Tell him I'll pay your salary and keep you on, so he'll know it's in good hands and the deal is straight. And tell him I'll make up my mind at the end of the month."

"Sure." Ira's eyes dropped away from her face and stared at their linked fingers. "But you don't have to go to all that trouble. Forget the lease and salary. He's a— gambler. He'll take a chance."

"No. I don't believe in free rides. If you get one, you end up paying in some other way. I want a business deal, proper insurance, everything honest and aboveboard."

Ira sighed, drawing in a deep breath and letting it out, his eyes still on their linked hands. "Okay, I'll start being honest and aboveboard. I own the boat, Sparrow."

After a moment she withdrew her hand from his and stood up. "It's late. Do you mind if we leave now?"

He glanced up and saw the anger and disappointment in her face. Grabbing her hand, he jerked her down again. "Listen! It's no big thing. After all, it was your assumption that I was a hired captain. I didn't lie."

"It's the same thing! You let me believe it." She looked away, breathing hard, conscious that she was actually trying to pump up more anger. He was right; it was no big thing. But she wanted to make it big, to tell herself it was stupid to go on with this, crazy to think she might find what she wanted . . . except now she knew he wasn't looking for a woman with money. He didn't need money. He didn't need her. "I suppose," she said, clenching her fists, "you had a good laugh at my stupidity."

"I did not! I . . ." He hesitated, staring at her. Honest, she had said. "Maybe I did think it was amusing at first," he added. "Is that so awful?"

She glanced at him. "You could have told me sooner. . . . Oh, forget it. I'm acting like a brat."

She stood up again, frowning, and he stood with her. Her face was still flushed, and the small, jagged scar over her left eye had pinkened, he could see a tiny vein pulsing there. On impulse he bent and kissed it, his touch feather light. "Come cruise with me, Sparrow."

She gave him a quick, amazed glance and turned away, shaken by the little caress. "All right. I do want to go. But not as your guest. I asked for a month's lease. . . ."

"No. It will be my pleasure."

"I won't go at your expense. I told you how I felt about free rides."

Ira shrugged. "We'll split, then." He grinned suddenly. "If you feel you can afford it, Ms. Roberts."

"I'll scrape it up," Diane said, dropping into dry humor, "one way or another."

They were laughing and talking, making plans, as they passed the boat where the party was going on. The crowd had grown, both in size and noise, and most of the guests ignored them. But one feminine voice squealed a greeting.

"Ira, baybee-e-e! When did you get back?"

Ira raised a hand in greeting, but didn't slow his pace. "Hi, Carol. Looking great, kid. See you around."

"Hey, wait a minute." The slender blonde rushed to the stern and tugged futilely at a line. "Come down here! You've got to join the party, party man." She was scrambling up onto the transom, stretching higher, when Big John grabbed her by the waist and pulled her back, down into the boat.

"Let him go, Carol Ann. He's got a date." He yelped as the blonde's high heel came down upon his bare foot. "Rosie, for the love of Mike, take this woman down in the cabin and give her a cup of coffee!"

Stepping off the dock and onto the sand path that ran around to the parking area, Diane took Ira's arm and looked up at him. It was dark, but the flaring, yellow arc lights flickered across her face and showed him the tilt of her smile. "Party man?"

He laughed and then sobered. "Used to be, I admit. Lots of gregarious people in marinas. And not much to do except have fun." He hesitated. "Like everything else, it gets old after a while."

"Everything else?"

He glanced down at her quickly. From some of the women he knew, that question would be provocative. From Diane Roberts it was plainly inquiring. She was studying him, figuring him out. It occurred to him that she might be rather good at that, after her years as CEO of the Stephan Corporation.

"That did sound jaded, didn't it? I expect I've spent too many years amusing myself and I'm tired of it. I think I need a change."

"That's why you considered selling your yacht, isn't it?"

Ira opened the car door for her, walked around and slid into the driver's seat before he answered.

"That's right. I've been bored as hell with my life. This cruise we're planning is the first thing I've looked forward to for a year or more."

Diane gave a disbelieving laugh. "That doesn't make sense, Ira. Aren't you tired of cruising, too? You must have had dozens of parties aboard that floating playroom."

"Parties, yes. But only when tied to a dock." Starting the car, he looked over at her quizzically. "My party friends don't ask me to take them out on the *Sea Fever*. They all know the liquor cabinet is locked before the engines turn over." He smiled at her startled look. "Does that bother you?"

"Not at all."

"I didn't think it would." Driving out, Ira fell silent, his attention on the traffic streaming past on the street ahead, his mind on the woman beside him. She struck him as being sure of herself as a person. But as a woman? He kept thinking of that overheated moment on the couch, when he'd damn near lost control. She had apologized, for God's sake! Claimed it was her fault, and *apologized*. As if she had gone too far; as if he had been repelled. She wasn't going to be easy to figure out.

"Ira?"

"Mmm?"

"If you'll give me a few hints, I'll be glad to shop in the morning for the supplies we'll need."

He shook his head. "I've done it so often, it's second nature for me. You pack your clothes, I'll provision the boat. Weather permitting, we'll leave at noon." They were on the bridge now, and he glanced over and saw that she was smiling, staring out across Biscayne Bay. As always, the bay was a giant, black mirror, reflecting the dazzling silver and gold, red and blue and green sparkles that showered light from the city of Miami, from the streaming rivers of cars, from the lights on the bridges, the lights of ships. Ripples coruscated with shattered brightness.

"I remember the open ocean at night," she said softly. "It was like black satin as far as you could see, gleaming with star shine."

Ira looked away. "Weather permitting," he said again, clearing his throat. "Remember that. Nothing is perfect. And the ocean is not always peaceful."

She nodded, but said nothing. Slotted into the bridge traffic, Ira drove by habit and thought about Diane. He had trouble seeing her as the daughter of Harrington Roberts, who was said to be so afraid of being kidnapped that he lived in a barricaded house and rode in an armored car. He glanced over again, seeing her profile etched by the dim light. A smooth brow, marred by that silly scar. A slight hump in an otherwise classic nose, full, nicely curved lips, a firm chin. She must have felt his gaze, he thought, for she turned to look at him. He smiled and looked forward again, easing off the bridge.

"What does your father think of you running around without guards? Does he worry?"

She leaned back and chuckled. "When I insisted on leaving the compound to go to college, my father took full page ads in *The Miami Herald*, the *Chicago Tribune* and *The New York Times*, saying that he was disowning his daughter and would not pay ransom if she were kidnapped."

Ira laughed. "You're putting me on."

"No, I'm not. He really did that. He's proud of the results."

"Results?"

Diane's eyes glinted as she glanced over. "Sure. No one has ever kidnapped me. Of course, Roberts is a common name, and frankly I don't think anyone knew he had a daughter until he ran the ads."

Ira nodded. "It sounds more as if he wanted to scare you into giving up your plans."

"Exactly." Diane stared ahead, her amusement fading. "And now he's at it again—trying to make me sell Yuri's house and move in with him. I'd rather be kidnapped."

"No problem," Ira said, stopping at the bronze gates. "I'll take care of that tomorrow." He blew his horn and raised his brows as the gates stayed stubbornly closed. "Uh-oh. No open sesame this time."

"Alycides fell asleep, I expect. Wait...." She slid out, touched a button on the gatepost, spoke quietly and slid back in, shutting the car door as the gates swung open. Driving through, Ira glanced at her curiously.

"Voiceprint?"

She smiled. "How did you know?"

"Instant result. How many voices does it recognize?"

"Now that Yuri is dead, only three. Mine, Anna's and Paul's. It's handy when Alycides dozes off."

"I see. Now that the house is yours, do you plan to have it reprogrammed?"

Diane shook her head. "They're friends, Ira. This will straighten out, I'm sure. It'll just take time."

Ira shrugged and drove on. She could be right. She knew Paul better than he did. But if he had to bet, he'd bet there would be trouble first.

5

AT DAWN Ira moved the *Sea Fever* to the service dock and
took on fuel and water. On a yacht this size these were
chores usually done by a mate, but since Ira valued his
privacy, he hired a mate only for long trips and fishing
tournaments.

That done, he went to the nearest shopping center and
bought supplies, running through a mental list so familiar he didn't have to think about it. He thought about
Diane Roberts instead.

Last evening he'd left her at the imposing entrance to
the Stephan home, refusing her invitation to come in for
a nightcap. It had been plain that Paul and the Brodor-
skis were gone, so she needed no help there. Besides, he
was wary of his own impulses. There was something
about the woman that really got to him; something he
couldn't describe, except that it made him want to protect her, to hold her, to know her in every way. He had
wanted to stay, but he'd left, saying he'd be back to pick
her up before noon the next day. She had smiled and said
no.

"Alycides will bring me down, and I'll be on time."

He believed her, mostly because of the stars in her eyes.
She was definitely high on this trip. She was as excited
as a kid. Carrying out the purchases and packing them
into the trunk of a rental car, he laughed. He was, too.
Of course, the feeling would go away, for her as well as

him, but after the boredom of the past few days, it was going to be wonderful while it lasted.

AT A QUARTER PAST ELEVEN Alycides brought a car to the entrance, frowned, and mounted the few steps to pick up the strapped, red and blue nylon bags waiting at the door. None of the servants liked Diane's plans, for the rumor was that Paul Stephan was going to court to take away everything his father had given Ms. Roberts, and that would include the house and affect their jobs. They felt she should stay at home and protect her interests. And theirs. Yuri had told them all they'd be safe with her.

Inside, Diane held a telephone to her ear and tapped a sandaled foot. She was dressed in white again; white slacks and a sleeveless, white pullover of knitted silk. "I know," she said. "I understand. But what can he do, Henry? The papers are signed." She listened impatiently. "Look," she broke in finally, "I've got to hang up and get going. Whatever Paul's planning in the way of trouble, he'll do it, whether I'm here or not. Just ride it out. He can't win. Goodbye, friend. I'll see you when I get back." She hung up and went swiftly to the door and out, hearing the phone ringing again as she ran down the steps.

"Ignore it," she called back to the maid. "I'm gone." She scrambled into the car, amazed at herself. Alycides started the quiet engine and drove away, his dark, ancient face stiff with disapproval. She felt a pang of guilt.

"He can't take the house," she said. "I checked. Stop worrying."

Some of the stiffness left the old man's face. "He will try, *hija*."

"He will fail."

"We will pray that is so." Alycides still sounded critical, but she could see him relax. He had been with Yuri for years, as had all the old servants. They thought of the sprawling estate as their home, though they knew Paul wanted to raze the big house and sell off the land. Yuri had known, too, which was why he had given it to Diane long before his death.

"It is so," she said gently. "Don't you think Yuri Stephan knew how to make out a deed? His home will always be your home, I promised him that. Of course, if you start stealing the silverware, I may change my mind...."

Alycides was still grinning as he pulled into the marina, while Diane, catching sight of Ira coming toward them from the docks, drew in her breath and was silent, conscious of a warmth and trembling in her middle. He looked wonderful. He was wearing shorts and a gold and white shirt that fitted him like a glove. His long, tautly muscled legs were bronzed by the sun and haloed by springing, golden hair. She looked away and got out as Alycides opened the door, then reached back in for the smallest of the bags before she turned and smiled.

"I'm not late, am I?"

He grinned, brushing against her as he reached past for the rest of the bags. "No." He nodded at Alycides, refused his offer of help with the bags and waited while Diane said goodbye to the old man. Then he led the way along the dock and Diane followed, conscious of the people lounging on the decks of other boats and of the interested glances that took in both the bags Ira was carrying and the woman behind him.

Clambering down to the deck of the *Sea Fever*, she saw that the chairs and small tables had been put away.

"Cleared for action?"

"Right. I expect good weather, but it can get rolly in the Stream." He picked up the bags again and went on. Diane followed close behind him, through the saloon and companionway, heading for the cabins below. In the lighted corridor he stopped suddenly and turned, looking down at her.

"Where do you want these?"

She had almost run into him. She teetered and caught herself with a hand on his arm, staring up at him in surprise. She had supposed he'd take it for granted that they'd sleep together, and while she'd been nervous, she'd been willing. But he wasn't? She looked away, feeling embarrassed, feeling spurned. He was silent, waiting patiently for an answer, and that made her feel worse. He probably had guessed at once that she had thought they'd share his bed. Her face hot, she moved around him, opened the first door and stepped inside for a closer look. The cabin was luxurious, the two beds and storage units built into the shining, teak walls, the dark blue rug soft and thick.

"This will be fine."

He stepped in behind her, put the bags down and unfolded a table fastened to the wall, setting its two legs firmly. He put the biggest of her bags onto the table and smiled at her. "My own invention," he said. "A seagoing luggage rack. Want to unpack and settle in? You've plenty of time. It'll be slow going until we're outside the Bay."

"Good idea." She kept her face averted, pretending an interest in the decorative prints on the wall. "I'll do that." She heard the door close quietly, a faint sound of footsteps receding, and turned to the full-length mirror beside the built-in drawers. "Fool!" she told herself vehemently, but was still relieved to see that her face was calm and a normal color.

In a few moments she heard the engines turn over and then a rumbling vibration as they warmed up. Quick excitement leaped in her veins. She quelled it by unpacking. Beneath her feet the deck moved. The yacht was sliding away from the dock, heading out.

As she worked, her mind cleared. In giving her a choice of where she would sleep, Ira had simply put the ball into her court. It was considerate, except that it would have been easier on her tender ego if he'd insisted on putting her into his bed immediately. She needed to know she was wanted.

Closing drawers, stowing the empty bags, she thought about going up and sitting with Ira in the wheelhouse. He probably expected it, but she still felt hesitant. *No,* she thought, *be honest.* What she felt was fear. The same old fear of being found inadequate. Anyway, for this question she had a precedent. On the chartered yachts the captains preferred to be alone at the wheel until they were through the crowded traffic in ports and inlets. She lay down on one of the bunks, thinking of Yuri and feeling lonely but stronger. She had made him a promise; now she was carrying it out. Looking for happiness. Looking for adventure. Taking a chance. What if she lost? She closed her eyes and refused to consider failure.

THE GULF STREAM was calm, a glittering, clear blue river traveling deep and fast to the north, its hurrying, riffling edges bordered by the greenish water of the Atlantic. In the Stream, the *Sea Fever* cut a slanting course to the northeast, running like a scared cat. With the automatic pilot set, the loran clicking off position and the radar screen keeping watch, Ira lounged back in his seat and took it easy. He'd pushed back the panels of glass on each side of the wheelhouse and the breeze blew in, rattling the charts in their rack, the plastic tumblers in their gimbals. He seemed oblivious to anything except the long, glittering plains of the sea before him, but turned, quick as a cat himself, as Diane came to the door behind him. She took the matching chair beside his.

"Eyes in the back of your head? I don't remember making any noise."

He had known she was there. He was a bit uneasy about it, wondering at her effect on him. "You didn't. For that matter, I couldn't have heard you in this racket if you had." He slid one window shut, bringing the rattle of charts down to an occasional crackle. "You've been sleeping?"

"How did you know?"

"You look relaxed." He ran his eyes over her, touching the long ripple of silky hair, the scar—why did that bother him so much?—the bump in her narrow nose, the sparrow bones and small breasts. He had known her legs were long, but in slacks they went on forever. His gaze traveled slowly up again and fastened on her mouth, remembering. He looked away, conscious of a strong, sexual reaction and shifted in his seat. "Are you hungry?"

She shook her head. "Not yet. Where are we?"

"About two and a half hours out of Freeport. We'll check in there and get our cruising permit, but unless you want to shop at the International Mall, we'll skip the island."

"I'm not much of a shopper."

"Good. That saves time for other things."

She started to ask what other things, but dropped it. "Where will we go from there?"

"Where would you like to go?"

She spread her hands, smiled and shrugged. "The Bahamas."

"I've a place you'll like on Eleuthera and some easygoing, noninterfering friends. There's a nice beach, a few horses." He raised his brows as she laughed. "What's funny?"

"A rider I'm not. I'm scared of horses. I can swim, but I'm not into other sports, unless you count skeet shooting. I do that, mainly because guns were my father's hobby. I know a lot more about guns than I want to. And about shooting."

Ira's brows went up again, but this time he smiled. "Great. I'm a shootist myself, and so are the Griffiths."

"The Griffiths?"

"My easygoing friends, Jack and Glenda. Glenda will give you a run for your money if you take her on at any kind of trapshooting. She's got the eye for it."

Diane gave him a cocky grin. "Me, too. It'll be the Superbowl of skeet. Have they got a range?"

"Sure."

"Plenty of guns? Small bore?"

Ira gave her a surprised look and then smiled. "I keep thinking you know everything about me, but of course you don't. I carry enough munitions aboard *Sea Fever* to start a small rebellion, including some fine skeet guns."

"Oh." Diane's smile had faded, her gaze, fixed on his face, had sharpened. "Maybe," she added slowly, "I should tell you I'm not into smuggling, either."

Ira frowned. "Don't jump to conclusions. I'm an arms dealer, licensed and bonded." His narrowed eyes swept her face. "Do I look like a smuggler to you?"

"No," Diane said sheepishly, "you don't. You look like a licensed and bonded arms dealer, righteously angry. But why bring the merchandise on vacation?"

He waved an arm. "This is my home. If someone wants to see a sample, I have one. Besides, guns are a hobby with me."

"I see." She fell silent, staring at the sea and the deepening blue of the afternoon sky to the east. The radar had been pinging for several minutes, and now she saw why. A good-sized sloop was ahead of them, tacking to the southeast. Diane watched Ira's hand move casually to override the autopilot and change the heading to a more northerly course. He saw her watching and grinned.

"We'd miss them anyway, but they wouldn't like our wake tossing their stern about."

"I suppose not." She hadn't really cared what he was doing; she had liked watching his hand. Large, with a broad palm, the long fingers agile and sure, touching the controls with an easy skill. When he had kissed her that night after that miserable dinner for Paul and Anna, his hands had moved over her in exactly the same way— gentle but skillful. And so warm. Thinking about it now gave her a shivery tremor of pleasant weakness. She stood up on shaky legs.

"I'm thirsty. Can I bring you something?"

"Orange juice, please."

"WE'LL ANCHOR OUT, once we're clear of the main traffic," he told Diane after they left the Grand Bahama harbor with their cruising permit. "Drinks and dinner aboard, if you don't mind."

"Maybe I should tell you I've never learned to cook."

Ira grinned, putting an arm around her waist. "That's one of the things I plan to teach you."

"Oh." Easing out of his grasp, she left the wheelhouse and went below to her cabin to freshen up. Teach her to cook? Why? But then, why not? It might be a useful skill—no, it *would* be a useful skill—out in the world of adventure. Brushing her hair, she laughed at the sheer silliness of what came immediately to mind. Jungles. Trekking across deserts. Shipwrecked on a tropical island. Lost in a wilderness. Lost, she admitted, in the land of make-believe. But who cared? This was fun, running away from gloom and doom and all those problems. Startled by the sound of a rattling anchor chain and the sudden cessation of engine noise, she put down the brush and ran out, feeling great, feeling young and foolish and happy, heading up to the galley for her first cooking lesson.

"POUR THE WINE, pass the goblets, bring out the cheese and sit down. This time you watch." The towel wrapped around Ira's waist slid free and dropped to the floor as he walked back and forth. Bending, Diane picked it up and put it around him again, tucking it into the top of his shorts. He grinned, wiggling his brows at her suggestively. She laughed, snatched her hands away from his taut warmth and went for the wine.

"What am I watching you make?"

"I forget—some French thing. It's good." He had started a pot of rice and was chopping carrots and onions, dumping them into a heavy saucepan, adding butter, setting it on a slow burner. "Takes a few minutes," he said and sat down, reaching for his goblet. "Do you like it?" he asked, indicating the wine. "Or would you rather have a martini?"

"I'm happy," she said, and pushed the plate of cheese toward him. "But I don't think I'm learning much. Are those lobster tails by the stove?"

Ira laughed. "Don't tell me you've never seen lobster tails before."

"I won't. How could I? We ate lobster together at the Neptune, remember? I love lobster. Are these as good as the red ones?"

Ira's eyes widened, his mouth twitched. "Better," he said gravely. "Much better. You'll see." *I'm happy*, she'd said, and she looked it. Her body was vibrant with excitement, her face open and responsive, the wariness gone. He reached over and covered her hand with his. "You look chirpy, Sparrow. It did you good to get away from Miami."

"Chirpy!" She leaned back and laughed helplessly. "What a way you have with words! Aren't you afraid you'll ruffle my feathers?"

Ira grinned and got to his feet. "I plan to put some meat over those bones instead."

She got up, too, coming around the table with her glass of wine to stand beside him and watch. He chopped the tails into chunks, leaving the shell on, and put them into a heavy skillet already sizzling with butter and olive oil. He kept the heat high, turning the chunks often, glancing at her as they turned red. Her brows went up. "Okay," she said, shrugging, "so I didn't know. Why didn't you tell me?"

"When it comes to teaching you things you ought to know, I'd rather show you. It's more fun."

She looked up at him and then away, warm and confused. "What's next?"

"Add stuff." He dumped in the carrots and onions, white wine, herbs, tomato sauce and fish bouillon. When the mixture boiled, he turned it down to simmer, checked the rice, and poured more wine into their glasses. "All right," he said and sat down. "Give it ten and then I'll take out the lobster, reduce the sauce and serve it all with the rice. Do you think you're learning anything?"

Diane slid into her chair and smiled. "I hope so. Did you know that stuff smells exactly like lobster Bordelaise?"

He groaned and slumped down in his chair. "I should have known you'd recognize it. You probably ate it in Bordeaux at a gourmet restaurant, right?"

"No," she said, "I've never been to France. I hope I didn't spoil your surprise."

He rose and stalked around the table, bent down and tipped up her head, his hands warm over her ears. "You're beautiful, Sparrow," he said huskily and kissed her, a long and lingering kiss that summed up the waiting he'd endured all day. In the middle of it he lifted her out of her chair and into his arms and pressed her full-length against him.

The kiss went on, easing into a gentle but thorough exploration, a slow tasting and breathing in, until it seemed to her that this kiss was more intimate than anything that had ever happened to her. And that she knew Ira Nicholson better than she had ever known any man before. Which was foolish, of course. There had been one she'd known entirely too well. She put her hands between them and eased away.

"Ira . . ."

He took a deep breath. "I know. Don't burn the dinner."

Or me. She sat down, immediately ashamed of the thought. All men weren't the same; she wasn't the same as she'd been eight years ago. "Yes. It would be awful to ruin something that good."

IRA BROUGHT OUT the deck chairs after dinner and a table for their coffee and brandy. The night was clear, the air soft, the southern stars seemed almost close enough to touch. The lights of Grand Bahama glittered behind them. At first, Diane tried valiantly to think of things to say, then gave up. The tension after that kiss had stayed through dinner and was still there—hanging like a force field of desire between them. Ira was no help. He sat there, nearly motionless, looking stern and saying nothing. Finally Diane moved. She rose, picked up the cups and empty glasses, took them into the galley and washed them. Then she found a towel and dried them. When she had finished, she turned and saw Ira lounging against the door. He smiled rather uncertainly.

"I finally thought of something brilliant to say," he said, and straightened. "Your place or mine?"

Diane stared. He looked rather pale, and a small muscle flickered nervously along his jaw. He seemed nine-tenths sure she'd make some excuse or turn him off with a flip remark. So he'd tried to protect himself by making it casual, as if he didn't care. But he did care. It was there in his eyes. He wanted her—he really did. As much as she wanted him. She turned away, suddenly dizzy with the knowledge. She tried to calm down, making a business of shaking out the dish towel and hanging it up.

"Yours," she said, finally, straightening the towel. "I'd like to try the Jacuzzi."

6

HE CARRIED HER down the narrow companionway, along the quiet corridor and into the master stateroom, letting her slide down his already aroused body and kissing her twice before he started to take off her clothes. Even so he was careful, almost too careful.

"I won't break," she murmured.

"You look like you might. Your skin is as delicate as silk." Easing up her pullover over her head, he stopped in midair and kissed her breasts, taking the nipples into his mouth. Her gasp was muffled, her face pink as her head emerged.

"That wasn't fair."

He laughed and lifted her so her breasts were level with his mouth and held her there while he kissed them again. She felt his tongue curl around a nipple, felt his heat, his sudden urgency and caught her breath, balancing her hands on his shoulders. "Ira, I . . ." She shut her eyes, feeling the stab of desire, the running, quivering flame that raced from breast to loin. "Oh, please . . . let me down. I want . . ."

"I want, too." He put her on her feet and stood looking at her, his hands cupping her shoulders, his strange eyes softened and dark. Taking a deep breath, he drew her to him again, his hands caressing the smooth, bared skin of her back, his cheek against her fragrant hair. "I've never wanted anyone else quite this much or in quite this way," he said huskily. "What have you done to me?"

There was no answer to that, and she didn't try for one. Instead she relaxed in his arms and put her hands under his loose shirt, drawing warm patterns around his waist and up, threading her fingers through the crisp hair on his chest, circling the flat nipples with her fingertips. In a minute his shirt was off; his shorts and her slacks and scrap of silk bikini joined the rest of the cast-off clothes on the floor.

"You're beautiful, Sparrow."

"So are you, darling. How did you get such a wonderful tan all over?"

He laughed unevenly and led her to the bed. "The usual way. There's a lot of privacy at sea." He reached with one hand to throw back the covers and then sank with her into luxurious, silk sheets. Diane turned in his arms and pushed herself up, looking down into his eyes. She seemed pale and serious. He smiled reassuringly and tried to pull her down. She stiffened against his arm.

"Wait . . . I mean, please listen a minute, Ira. I should have said this before." She straightened again as he let her go. "It's only fair that I tell you that I . . . that I'm not very good at this, and if it's not . . . not exactly what you expect, it's not your fault."

He stared up into the intense blue eyes. "I see," he said. "If what we achieve is not perfection, it's all your fault."

She dropped back into the curve of his arm and shut her eyes. "Don't. Don't make fun of me. Maybe I shouldn't have said it, but I'd rather tell you than have you find it out for yourself. I—I'm really a lousy lover."

"How do you know that?"

She opened her eyes. "I was told by someone who knew. Look, I didn't want to start a discussion group— I just wanted to warn you. All right?"

The blue eyes now looked shamed and desperate. Rolling, Ira put both arms around her, captured her tense mouth with his, nudged her lips apart and burrowed in.

She let him do whatever he wanted to do; it was what a man expected. She kissed him back, awkwardly, closing her eyes and waiting for the rest of it. But he kept on kissing her, moving over her face with light little licks, teasing her ears until she shivered with desire. Then he went back to her mouth.

"Now," he breathed, "I want it all." He kissed her with a subtle thoroughness that demanded surrender. In a moment her mouth relaxed and she sighed, drawing in his hot breath, tasting the essence of an aroused male, reacting with a rush of heat, a feeling of liquid pooling deep inside.

"Oh, Ira . . . oh, darling." She moved beneath him, trembling, stroking his tight buttocks with feverish hands. "Tell me what you like," she whispered when he drew back. "Tell me how to please you."

"You please me," he whispered, "you don't need any lessons." His hands moved over her, hard bronze over ivory silk. Hungry hands, but gentle, wise about giving pleasure. She tried, still awkward and uncertain, to return his caresses, to stroke him in all the places she could reach, but as he went on with his lovemaking her hands shook and grew weak. Her breasts ached with exquisite pain when he suckled, her slim hips moved involuntarily as desire became a fever. He slid a hand beneath her and cupped a hip. "Padded velvet," he murmured. "Not skinny there, are you?"

She smiled, but couldn't answer him. She was hot all over, his hand caressing her was driving her crazy. She *wanted*, hopelessly. This was the worst of it; it had always been like this. She remembered too well. And this time was worse. She had never wanted with such burning intensity.... Oh, *what* was he doing? His hands, his mouth ... She drew in her breath and went still, as still as a statue, hardly breathing. Then she moaned, raising her hips, pushing up against the subtle, teasing pressure on the tiny point of her desire, pushing up again and then again. Subsiding, she looked at his dark, dimly lighted face in panting amazement. He smiled, his tiger eyes gleaming.

"Touch me," he said, and guided her hand to his tautly straining shaft. "Take me where I want to be."

As in a dream she caressed him, took him into both her hands and made a cradle of her thighs to receive him. Silently she coaxed him over her and drew him down. He paused there, holding back, wanting to enter her slowly, gently. He fought his urgency, willed himself control, and then slid his hands beneath her hips to raise her to his thrust.

"I'll be easy, little one."

His voice was hoarse, choked with passion. Her eyes were dark and dazed, her mouth soft. When he spoke she didn't seem to hear him. Then slowly her expression changed to one of awe.

"I made it," she said softly, wonderingly. "I really made it when you touched me like that. That never happened to me before. It felt wonderful."

"Wait," he got out, as much to himself as to her. "Just ... wait." He entered her, and for the first time in years, could hardly breathe for the pounding of his heart.

She was with him from the first; excited, trembling, full of rippling passion, taking him in and wrapping her slender legs around his thighs as if she'd never let him go. And then, when the rhythmic movement came to a peak, when the bright tension shattered into dark, pulsing ecstasy, she gasped and slipped her hands to his buttocks again. She held him there in desperate hunger until the thrumming, beating waves of exquisite pleasure dissolved into a languorous glow.

Breathless from the glorious completion that had swept them away, Ira moved to her side. "All my life," he managed to say, "I've been looking for something without knowing what it was."

Her eyes still shut, Diane lay still, refusing to move and chance destroying this dream. "What was it?"

"A lousy lover." He said it with infinite satisfaction.

Her eyes flew open and she sat up, looked down at him and laughed—softly, murmurously, the laugh that always made him want to kiss her. Collapsing onto his chest, she put her arms around him, her cheek on his shoulder. "You're wonderful, you know that? A wonderful man, who has given me a wonderful gift. You've got your lousy lover for the duration."

He heard the shaky wonder in her voice. She was a lovely, passionate woman. What kind of a man—or men—could make her believe she was frigid, make her feel inadequate in bed? He would find out. Somehow he would make her tell him, get it out and get it over with. But for now he pulled her closer and kissed her ear. "The duration of what?"

"The adventure."

"And how long is that?"

She yawned and tightened her arm around his waist. "I don't think there's a set time for adventure, darling. I think you just know when it's over."

He rubbed his cheek against her silky hair, his smile fading. He'd been dumb to ask. He never asked. He never wanted anything to last beyond the initial attraction, and he certainly didn't want to trail around behind a woman as rich as this one. Sometimes something wonderful came long, but it always went along, too. He thought about that for a moment, then drew her hair away from her ear and whispered into it. "Now do we try this in the Jacuzzi?"

FIRST LIGHT had turned the portholes a pearly gray when Diane awoke the next morning. She lay still, absorbing the feeling of a new day, of the gentle rocking of the yacht, the miracle of sensual satisfaction and the sight of Ira sprawled beside her, utterly male and beautiful. She let her gaze travel the room. The smoked mirrors on the walls gave back a myriad of dim images—her tangled hair and sleepy face, his bronzed and muscular body— the open door behind them and the edge of the shining, black tub beyond. She couldn't help thinking how luxurious and suggestive the stateroom was, with its acre of bed, its thick rugs and concealed lighting, the deep chairs and a state-of-the-art stereo. A bachelor's dream, she thought. No doubt she was the latest in a long line of appreciative women.

She sighed, dreams fading, then carefully slid from the bed and eased the door open, heading along the corridor to her own stateroom and straight into the shower. She was dressed in shorts and a pullover and drying her hair when Ira came looking for her. He was wearing a towel and a stubble of beard.

"So, this is where you are." He seemed a little irritated. She wished he'd waited until she'd finished dressing. Without corrective makeup, the jagged scar on her forehead shone a brilliant, ugly pink after a shower and shampoo. But she smiled brightly.

"Good morning. If you'll tell me how to make coffee, I'll go up and start it while you shave."

His irritation faded as he stood there, looking at her. She had drawn away from the closeness of the night. She was still wary under that smile. He was more disappointed than irritated. He had wanted to waken with her in his arms.

"I'll make the coffee, Sparrow. I'll be right up."

He was gone, heading for his room before she could argue. She looked into the mirror and shook her head. What difference did it make? He knew what she looked like. He knew how she was in bed—awkward and eager. He'd seemed to like it, but maybe he just liked novelty. Maybe he'd go on liking novelty for long enough. She refused to consider how long, or short, that might be.

By nine Ira had radioed a message to the Griffiths and the *Sea Fever* was running free for Eleuthera, both engines wide open, a rooster tail of spray rising from the blue water behind them, the loran madly clicking off a blur of numbers. This was where the vessel shone; she was built and powered for speeds impossible in most boats her size. Feet up, Ira lazed back at the wheel, watching the sea and occasionally glancing over at Diane in her chair. She seemed so calm, so cool, sitting there. But silent. Too silent, all morning. He'd hoped— he wasn't sure what he'd hoped for, but it wasn't silence.

"We're traveling deep water here," he said offhandedly, "we can make good time. Once we're close to the islands, it's often shallow and tricky and we have to creep."

Diane looked at him and smiled. "I've been wondering about the Griffiths."

"Oh. They're easygoing, like I said. Around fifty, kids grown and gone. They've got a place near Governor's Harbour where they live most of the time, and a guest house that's mine when I want it. Beautiful spot, with a nice beach."

Diane looked down at her hands. "Are you going to tell them who I am?"

He was silent a moment. "I told them your name," he said finally, "but that's all. If you want them to know more, you tell them. Gossiping is not one of my vices, nor theirs."

"Good."

"Do you trust anyone at all, Sparrow?"

"Of course," she said soberly. "I trust you to tell me the truth. But unless I ask, I don't know what you might find interesting enough about me to repeat to others. Had you said you would tell them I was Harrington Roberts's daughter, I would have asked you not to, that's all."

His broad mouth straightened. "What if I told them you were Yuri Stephan's live-in woman?"

She tossed her head. "I wouldn't mind. A lot of people thought that, and Yuri thought it was the joke of the century." She turned and looked at Ira. "He loved me. He was the only person who ever loved me. I lost my real father when Yuri died."

How could he be jealous of an old man, a dead man? He'd asked himself that once before, and there was still no answer. He shifted in his seat. "It's hard to believe parents could feel anything but love for their child," he said finally. "I realize your father is an eccentric, but your mother . . ."

"Died in childbirth."

"All right," he said almost harshly and sat up, reaching for the controls. The yacht slowed, mushing down, the stern rising and falling again as the wake washed forward. Ira eased the throttles into low speed and settled back again. "There has to be someone in your past," he continued, "someone or something that made you hide away with an old man. Tell me."

Braced in her seat, apparently surprised and confused by his words and actions she stared at him, her eyes startlingly wide and blue. Then she flushed, her cheeks going patchy red. "My past has nothing to do with you, Ira. It's over. You don't need to know anything about it."

"Yes, I do. If we're going to be friends, if we're going to be lovers, I need to know what hurt you."

Hesitantly she glanced up at him and then away. She wanted to believe she could be both of those things to him, to him and no other, but that was like believing in fairy tales or in Yuri's kind of love. Staring out at the sea, she tried to believe it was possible and failed. "I, well, I'm not sure I trust you that much."

His jaw set, Ira shook his head. "You either trust someone or you don't. Make up your mind."

"It's a boring story, Ira."

"Bore me."

She sighed and grimly gathered her thoughts. "You're going to keep on, aren't you? All right, remember you asked for it. It's not just boring, it's ugly. I was young and stupid. I fell in love with the wrong man, got pregnant, lost the baby and—and had a mental breakdown. That's it."

He stared at her silently for a full minute. Then he set the engine throttles at an idle and leaned back in his chair. "I believe you," he said. "Tell me the rest."

"That's all there is."

"What was the man's name?" He watched the flicker of pain in her eyes, the thinning and compressing of her lips.

"Ben Clifton," she said. "What difference does it make?"

"Why was he the wrong man?"

"Dammit! If you have to know, I'll tell you the whole filthy mess! I went to college under a different name, and so, when Ben asked me out, I thought he was actually falling in love with me, not my father's money. He was good-looking, and even when he found out I was really dumb about sex, he said he didn't mind. I had an apartment off campus and he moved in with me. I got pregnant right away. He said he was pleased and we'd get married as soon as he graduated."

Ira kept his gaze on the gently rolling sea, his thoughts black with illogical jealousy. "So far," he said neutrally, "that doesn't sound too bad. When did it go wrong?"

"Right after that. One day when Ben was in class and I wasn't, my father arrived." She stopped, then went on in the tone of pained mockery she always used when she spoke of her father.

"You've seen that grandstand play on TV, haven't you? The stretch limo, the four guards, the nurse? He sent one of the guards into the apartment house to get me, and when I came out he gave me an ultimatum. Either I gave up Ben immediately and came home to stay, or he'd disown me."

Ira glanced at the strained look on her face. He knew her well enough now to know what she had done. "You opted to stay with Ben."

"Of course. I told my father that Ben and I could make our own way. All he said was that I could come home when the affair blew up in my face." She swallowed, sliding her eyes away from Ira's quick look of surprise. "He already knew it would blow and it did. So I went home, and after a while I got to know Yuri, who was one of father's few friends, and asked him for a job. Now you know the story of my life."

"Tell me about when it blew."

She turned her head slowly and met his gaze. "I'd rather not."

"I know." He reached for her hand. "Have you ever told anyone the whole story?"

"I told Yuri."

"Then you can tell me." His eyes were warm now, gentle but insistent. Diane's resolve wavered. Maybe he would understand.

"All right. But you're asking a lot. When Ben came home, he asked if my father had been there. Ben had known who I was and he'd written to my father, threatening scandal about the baby unless my father agreed to our marriage and settled millions on us. Anyway, when he found out what I'd said and done, he was furious. He told me to call and apologize, to beg Father to take us in. I refused, and we had an awful fight. I—I accused him of making love to me because of my father's money, and he said I was . . . was damn well right, and I ought to thank him. He said I was a skinny, frigid piece of goods that no one in their right mind would want, except for Roberts's billions." Chin up, eyes wet but direct, she looked at Ira and dared him to comment. Ira squeezed her hand.

"You know better," he said softly. "Go on. Spill it all."

She swallowed. "There's not much more. I told him to save his pity and get out, and he . . . he lost his temper."

Ira let go of her hand and touched her scar. Her forehead was sheened with perspiration. "He did this?"

"Yes." This time Diane gave him her hand as he reached for it again. Her fingers trembled as she curled them around his. "He did...more. He beat me, broke my nose and one arm, and knocked me to the floor. Then he kicked me, over and over again. I lost consciousness. When I came to he was gone, and my neighbor was there with the police and a doctor. The doctor told me later that if the neighbor hadn't heard the fight and called the police, I would have died from internal bleeding. My—my baby did die."

His throat thick with anger and pity, Ira stood up, pulling her with him and holding her tightly. "I'm sorry, Sparrow. You went through hell, and I just put you through it again. But I'm honored that you trusted me enough to tell me."

She pulled away and sat down again, wiping at her eyes. "I wouldn't have, if you hadn't insisted. I'm not exactly proud of being such a fool."

"Stop blaming yourself! He was a cruel and vicious liar. You weren't at fault."

"I know that now. But I'm still afraid of making another mistake. Obviously I'm not very smart about men." She moved away, squaring her shoulders, and stared out at the sea, at the dim outline of land to the east. "Is that where we're going?"

He laughed abruptly and sat down at the wheel. "Right now I'm not sure where you and I are going."

7

LATE AFTERNOON, they anchored in Governor's Harbour in the lee of Cupid's Cay. Leaning on the rail, Diane stared fascinated at the tiny settlement on the Cay. It seemed to be composed of ruins.

"That," Ira said, coming up behind her, "is history. The oldest known, permanent British community in the Bahamas. Settled a couple of hundred years ago by a bunch of people who called themselves Eleutherians, after the Greek word for freedom." He faced her, leaning his back against the rail, and grinned. "No, I'm not making it up, Consider that you've found freedom, too. Ah, there comes Jack in his dinghy."

He was looking past her, so she turned and looked at the opposite shore. Weaving toward them through the other anchored yachts was a sturdy man in a yellow dinghy. Her eyes lifted from him to sweep the impossibly blue and white and gold world around them. There were people aboard most of the yachts, dressed in shorts or bikinis. Some were sunbathing, some were gathered in deck chairs to drink and talk or eat. All of them looked as if they hadn't a care in the world. Playtime. Her gaze dropped again to the man rowing toward them and saw he was drawing close.

"Where's your bag?"

Diane's gaze shot back to Ira's questioning face. "We're going with him now?"

"Sure. Glenda will be expecting us for dinner."

"Oh! All I have besides a bathing suit is one skirt and some shorts and blouses."

"Good. It won't take you long to pack." He laughed as her brows drew together. "Seriously, love, that's all you need."

Packing, Diane relaxed. He was probably right. Actually, she was sure of it. Ira was too kind to put her into a position she would find uncomfortable. Wearing shorts and a loose, colorfully embroidered blouse, and carrying one small bag along the corridor to the companionway, the depression she had felt since she'd talked about the past lifted and gave way to a feeling of expectancy; something good was going to happen. Stepping into the saloon, she saw Ira sitting with Griffith. Ira's gaze met hers; the gold-brown, tiger eyes warm and approving. She lifted her chin and smiled, thinking Yuri had been right.

Jack Griffith's skin was the color of mahogany, making his silver hair and light blue eyes startlingly bright. Short and broad, he stood up and offered his hand as she came up to them.

"Diane, I'm delighted. Usually we get this ornery cuss by himself. It's nice to have someone pretty around."

"I'm really glad to be here." She was. There was nothing but friendliness in his eyes; no speculation, no fawning, not even curiosity. She wasn't Harrington Roberts's daughter here, nor Yuri Stephan's live-in woman. She was just Ira Nicholson's new friend.

She thought about that as Jack rowed them back to shore. She sat on polished, wooden slats that formed the rear seat, her bare legs stretched out, warm from the afternoon sun, her eyes on the shore ahead. The hilly slopes that led up to the town of Governor's Harbour were blazing with the fiery red of royal poinciana blooms, like patches of flame flickering against the blue sky.

"Impressed, Sparrow?"

Her eyes went past Jack's thick shoulders to Ira, sitting on the bow to balance the small boat, and saw that he was watching her instead of the scenery.

"Of course. Will we stay in that town?"

He shook his head. "We'll be staying a few miles south, on a small bluff overlooking the ocean. Away from the crowds."

Jack laughed, resting on the oars. "Crowds? Compared with Nassau we have no crowds. Anyway, it's June. A good many of the Governor's Harbour residents are leaving for the summer. It'll be quiet as a church in another two weeks."

"We'll stay and see," Ira said.

At the docks they left the dinghy with an attendant and walked up to a shell road and a parked Jeep. They drove past the outskirts of the town, which looked more like New England than a tropical-island settlement. Many of the residences were white clapboard houses with Victorian gables, with well-tended emerald lawns. The town was small; the buildings thinned out and disappeared as they went southeast.

Jack drove with their luggage piled in the seat beside him, Ira sat with Diane in the back and held her hand, his grip casual but warm. Jack pointed out local sights to Diane.

"Glenda's looking forward to this," he ended, turning off into a lane bordered by a low, coral rock wall and tall trees. "Ten minutes after you radioed, Ira, she had the skeet guns out to shine them up." He caught Diane's surprised look in the rearview mirror and laughed. "She loves to shoot. But she may be off a bit. It's been months since she practiced."

"Not to worry," Diane said. "It's been years for me." She hadn't heard what Ira had said to Jack on the VHF, but clearly he'd tried to provide her with the only sport she knew.

As the Jeep slowed, Diane took in the sight wordlessly. Nothing Victorian here. A large, rambling house of wood and pinkish stone, giant palms casting pools of shade, riotous pink and purple bougainvillea that climbed low walls enclosing a swimming pool and tennis court. The view beyond was blocked by the house, but she could hear the ocean rumbling and smell the salt breeze.

"Where's the guest house?" she asked Ira, looking around.

"Over there," he answered, pointing south. "On a higher bluff, overlooking the sea. We'll leave the luggage in the Jeep and drive to it after dinner."

"There you are!" A woman emerged from the shadowed loggia surrounding most of the house, stepping into the sunlight and smiling. Diane smiled back involuntarily. The woman had to be Glenda. She was a perfect match for Jack—strongly built, deeply tanned, blue-eyed. A patch of matching silver streaked through her dark hair. She was friendly, Diane thought as Ira introduced them, and pleasant.

"I'm thrilled to have you here," Glenda said. "This is the first time in two years I've had someone to shoot with. Ira's too good for me." She looked at Ira and grinned. "The show-off uses a rifle for skeet. All right, you two, come on in. Drinks on the beach, then dinner."

Later, lounging in a canvas sling chair, full of wine and cheese, Diane watched the setting sun paint a rose-colored afterglow on clouds to the east. Ira and Jack were barefoot and walking along the wet sand washed by gentle waves, talking. She glanced at Glenda, who had begun to gather up glasses, and climbed out of the sling.

"I'll help. Since you and Jack were kind enough to let us come here, I want to do everything I can."

"Let you?" Glenda laughed. "That's like Ira. He didn't tell you this place is his, did he? We're just the caretakers, and darn glad we've got the job."

"Oh. Well, fine. But I still want to help."

Glenda stared and then smiled. "Follow me. Dinner's a casserole and salad. All we have to do is the table."

"LIKE FAMILY," Diane marveled later, walking out with Ira into a breezy, moonlit night and turning toward the dim shape of the Jeep. "Or at least like I believe most families must be. I feel completely at home with them."

"I'm glad. They're some of the good guys." Ira sounded relaxed, easy. In the moonlight he looked huge, Diane thought, huge and protective, his arm around her, his hand resting lightly on her waist as they approached the vehicle. She stood quietly while he took the bags from the front seat and threw them in the back, then climbed in, waiting in silence until he started the motor and turned it around.

"This is a beautiful place," she said, looking back at the house. "How long have you owned it?"

Leaving the parking lot by way of a narrow lane that led off to the south, Ira gave her a quick glance and then shrugged. "Four years. I bought it as much for Jack and Glenda as for myself."

"Why?"

Ira glanced at her again. He couldn't keep from looking at her. He was already sorry he'd brought her here so soon; he would have had her to himself on the yacht. The last hour of conversation, even with people he liked, had seemed like an eternity. He brought his mind back to her question and explained.

"Jack was my mate in my tournament-fishing days, and gave me some help when I developed a line of equipment. It sold well. I figured I owed them a place to live and an income."

"I see." Unconsciously she moved closer, drawn by the warmth she sensed in him. "Do you come here often?"

He waited a moment before answering, his attention on the curving lane, overhung with oleander branches. Their pink blooms released a sweet, subtle fragrance as the Jeep pushed through. "Twice, maybe three times a year. I never stay long."

"Why not?"

He shrugged again. "Restless, I suppose. Always looking for something new."

Diane nodded. That should be warning enough, she thought, to keep any woman from making long-range plans about Ira. Not that she would have. She had realized early that he was a—a what? A free soul? But then, so was she.

"There," Ira said as they rounded a curve, "is where we sleep. No one will bother us. Even the beach is private."

The headlights revealed a small, low house of weathered wood and large windows. As they drove nearer and parked, she saw the dark gleam of the ocean below, and remembered Ira saying the house was on a bluff. When he switched off the noisy engine, she could hear the sigh of the small waves, like the rustle of silk across a floor. She smiled and swung herself out, reaching to grab her bag.

Inside, Ira turned on the lights and left her there to go
back out and park the Jeep. Diane wandered through the
house, fascinated. Everything but the toilet and bath was
in one big room, with walls that appeared to be made of
driftwood, and handwoven rugs on the floor. A big bed,
big, plump chairs, bookcases, a stereo. A kitchen with
stainless-steel appliances, a dining table with four chairs,
an enormous bowl of fresh fruit. Seeing that, she checked
the refrigerator. Loaded. Eggs, bacon, ham, milk, butter, honey, bagels and what looked like homemade
bread. So, breakfast here. She turned as Ira came in and
saw him pause at the door, his eyes sweeping the room,
centering on her, staying on her as he came forward,
sleek as a big cat in spite of his size. The light from the
low lamps made his moving shadow immense on the
driftwood walls. She suddenly felt his tension and her
heart came up in her throat, pulsing there while she tried
to think of something to say.

"This is, uh, fine," she managed to say, moving out of
his path. "Really a nice place...." She stopped, facing
him, waiting.

She looked wary again, uncertain. He knew a moment of doubt and pushed it away. She would know
sooner or later that he would never hurt her. He came to
her without answering her remark and took her into his
arms, his hands slipping down to her hips and pulling her
tight against his thighs. He was hot and fully aroused. "I
want you," he said softly. "Right now. I was ready to grab
you and run an hour ago."

She drew in her breath, feeling her body melt against
him, shocked into intense desire by his heat and hardness, his passion. She lifted her mouth to him, and in the
middle of the kiss he lifted her, sliding an arm beneath
her thighs, cradling her against his chest like a child. She

dragged her mouth from his, put her arms around his shoulders and held on as he carried her to the bed.

"You'll think I'm crazy," he muttered, still holding her as he sat on the edge of the bed, "and you may be right." He looked into her eyes, his own strange eyes golden hot with piercing desire. It seemed to Diane that he was entering her with that searching gaze, looking for answers.

"No," she said, stroking his cheek, "not crazy. Or...maybe we both are." Suddenly flaming, she curled her arms around his neck and kissed him, licking his lips open with the tip of her tongue, wanting inside to taste him. He groaned and laid her on the bed, covering her with his chest, making the kiss his with his invading tongue, which thrust and thrust again in a rhythm that made her ache inside, made her arch against the hot, lean body close to hers. His hand ran down to her bare thigh, his fingers pressed beneath the edge of her tight shorts and a growl rose in his throat.

"Clothes." He muttered the word like an imprecation. "Let's get these things off...."

In no time they were knitted together but lying still, staring into each other's eyes, prolonging the moment as long as they could. Braced on his elbows, Ira held her head between his palms, tipped her chin up and now, having invaded her body with fire, invaded her mouth, slowly, gently, with his hot tongue.

She gasped and rippled beneath him, wanting, wanting more, wanting everything ... and then finding it, in his thrusting, tireless body, feeling it, growing and growing until it filled her, bursting into brilliance at last, spiraling bright colors like flowers in the darkness of her closed eyes, sending the sensation that was like no other pouring through her veins. So fast, she thought, dazed. Like beautiful, ecstatic lightning....

"Crazy!" The word gusted from Ira's panting mouth. He sat up, shaking his head, puzzled. "What is this with us? We aren't kids." He stared down at her flushed face, and when she opened her eyes and smiled, he caught her up against him and buried his face in her hair. "Sparrow... I can't get enough of you, and I don't know why. I don't even know why being with you keeps getting better. Tell me what's happening."

She shook her head and curled against him, content. She didn't know why and didn't care, as long as it lasted. Lasted, that is, long enough. She still didn't know just how long that would be, for it was too early, she told herself, to tell. Later she would know. Like you always knew when a dream came to an end. When you woke up. In the meantime, there was the rest of the night....

"I HAVE ALWAYS SAID that to wake up to the smell of perking coffee and frying bacon is to know heaven on earth. I thought you didn't know how to cook." His hair on end, his chin dark with beard, Ira sat up in bed and grinned at her.

She turned from the stove and laughed, looking proud of herself. "You showed me how to make coffee, remember? And the package of bacon had directions...." She picked it up and read: "'Use cold skillet to start, turn frequently, drain on paper towels.' Nothing hard to do there."

"Know anything about eggs?"

"Mmm, yes. They're full of cholesterol. How about something called toaster pancakes? There's a package of them in the freezer."

He sighed and crawled out of bed, heading for the bathroom. "You leave the eggs to me, Aunt Jemima. I have a severe cholesterol deficiency."

They ate hugely. Bacon and scrambled eggs and pancakes, and butter and strawberry jam. "Like gluttons," Ira said and sighed, finishing his coffee. "Like pigs."

"We just have healthy appetites," Diane insisted, and he nodded. His appetite for her was healthy enough; he could feel it stir as he watched her pink tongue curl around a jam-stained finger. "Maybe," she added, "we ought to go swimming and get some exercise."

"Fine. As soon as we clean this up." He stood, picked up his dishes and took them to the sink. Bringing her dishes, she followed him and copied every move he made, scraping, rinsing, fitting everything into the dishwasher, watching like a hawk as he added soap and shut and locked the door panel. Amused at her concentration, he stepped back and pointed at the starter button. "Push that."

She stepped forward and pushed, gingerly, then smiled at the sound of surging water. "I've always wondered about dishwashers," she said. "I've never seen one working. Too bad there isn't a window." She glanced up. "Stop grinning. It really is interesting. Think of the engineering, the creative thought it took.... All right, put me down! I'll get my suit."

"I'm having a window put in," Ira decided, carrying her out of the kitchen space. "Then I'll move the chairs in here, with a snack table between, and we'll watch your favorite programs. The Crystal Waterfall, The Dance of the Knives, Waltzing Bubbles. I never knew before how easy it was to entertain a real-estate magnate."

"I said put me down!"

He dropped her onto the unmade bed and leaned over her, a hand braced on each side, his eyes gleaming. "Are you sure you want to go swimming?"

She laughed, her indignation disappearing. "Yes. I want to go swimming. First, that is."

"That's better."

Wooden steps slanted down the short but steep bluff, a thatched shelter held a couple of benches and a table in the middle of a patch of pinkish sand. The Atlantic sent foot-high ruffles of blue water, edged with white foam lace, to tease them into wading. Holding hands, they sloshed through the waves and kept going until they were waist deep.

"Picture perfect," Diane said, surveying the sunlit sea and the empty beach. "Almost too perfect. Should I watch for currents?"

"No. Just watch out for me. Those two scraps of black nylon you're wearing would fit in my pocket."

"They'd better not!" She plunged in, slid beneath the surface and came up again twenty feet away. He had watched her every move in the glass-clear water, but was still surprised. She swam like a seal. He remembered she'd said that she only knew two sports, swimming and shooting.

"If you shoot as well as you swim," he said, grinning across the space between them, "you're championship material."

She laughed, squeezing water out of her hair. "I shoot even better than I swim."

Ira's brows went up. She sounded a touch arrogant. "How do you rate yourself on modesty?"

She laughed again, moving toward him. "Low. Very low." She still looked fragile, but now he could see it was mostly her delicate bone structure that gave that effect.

Muscles moved smoothly beneath her fair skin as she put her hands onto his chest and stroked upward, joining her fingers at the back of his neck. "I've never had much to be proud of," she added, suddenly serious, "so I brag when I can."

Looking down, taking in the clear blue eyes, starred with wet, spiked lashes, the jagged scar, the crooked bump in her aristocratic nose and the wide, but firmly contoured mouth, Ira was struck with incredulous wonder. It had come to him that there was only one answer that explained the way he felt about Diane Roberts. One unreasonable answer. This woman, probably the least perfect physically of all the women he'd known intimately, undoubtedly the one with the most serious problems, and certainly the one who had the most money—too much money—was the *one*. He was falling—had fallen—in love with her.

His hands, resting easily on her supple waist, tensed and began to tremble. He let her go.

"So, swim," he said abruptly. "That's why we came out here, isn't it?" He began swimming himself, heading straight out, slicing through the water toward the horizon.

Sometime later he felt a swirl beneath his body and she popped up in front of him. He slowed, trod water and stared at her. She smiled, smoothing a lock of hair out of her eyes.

"So, where are we going? Spain?"

He glanced behind them, seeing across a glimmering stretch of blue the distant line of shore, the outline of the bluff, the roof of the guest house. It all seemed very far away.

"Good God! Why didn't you say something?"

"For all I know," Diane said reasonably, "this is your normal workout. Want to start back?"

"Of course!" He looked at her carefully, searching for signs of fatigue. "Stay close, now, and when you tire you say so, immediately. Understand?"

She opened her mouth, closed it and nodded. She stayed within his arm's length all the way back to shore, though he did notice she had to slow her pace occasionally to let him catch up.

8

"SKEET THIS AFTERNOON?" Glenda, dishing out fresh-fruit salad for lunch, smiled as Diane nodded. "Great! I've got a 20-gauge you can use, or, of course, a 12-gauge."

"I'll take the twenty. Lazy, I guess."

Glenda raised her brows. "And I'd guess you're too good for me. The small bore makes it harder."

"I've a twenty-eight on the boat," Ira broke in. He gave Diane a challenging look. "It's a bit on the fine side, but you might be able to hit with it." He grinned as he saw her eyes narrow, her chin come up. She was rising to the bait.

"I'll take a look at it. Maybe I'll use it and beat your score." She noticed that except for an amused twitch at the corner of his mouth, Ira looked unperturbed.

After lunch, Ira and Jack took off for Governor's Harbour and Diane helped Glenda with clearing away.

"We'll stack them," Glenda said. "I'll finish up later."

Diane shook her head. "Let's do it now. I need the practice."

Glenda laughed. "Oh, sure. Be serious, Diane."

"I am being serious. I'm trying to learn."

"Oh?"

"Yes. I know it's stupid, but I never tried any of this."

Glenda stared and then shrugged. "So, your family had servants. You've always lived at home?"

"Why, no. I lived alone when I went to college, but just for a short time."

Glenda laughed. "What did you do about dishes, then?"

"We . . . I ate out," Diane said, feeling color come up into her face. "I don't know how to cook, either. I want to be able to take care of things myself."

"Well, sure. Everyone ought to learn to do things when it's necessary. What kind of work are you in?"

"I've been in real estate," Diane said, purposely vague, and went on scraping plates. "But I want a change."

"What are you considering?"

Diane's hands slowed and stopped. She put the last plate into the dishwasher and stood there, thinking of how to put into words the way she really felt. "Something worthwhile. Maybe, if I can learn enough to get in, the Peace Corps."

Glenda looked pained. "There's no money in that, Diane."

"I don't need money."

"Oh." For a moment Glenda seemed at a loss, then she gave a short laugh. "In that case, obviously you can do whatever you want to do. Even if it's nothing."

Diane was carefully measuring the detergent for the dishwasher. Pouring it into its container, she shook her head. "No, thanks. I know where that leads." She shut and locked the door panels, studied it a moment and then pushed the Start button. "There. Did I do that right?"

Glenda ran a hand through her silver-streaked hair and laughed again. "If you're thinking Peace Corps, you'd better learn how to wash dishes by hand. And I'll lend you a cookbook. Now let's go down to the range. Jack will bring stuff when they get back, but he hates to do the setup. I'll do that."

Hidden from the house by trees and shrubs, the range lay close to the edge of the bluff and overlooked a section of the property's private beach. Safe enough, Diane thought, for no one would be strolling there.

While Glenda loaded the clay disks, first in the high house and then the low, and set the mechanisms that threw them out, Diane paced the field, stopping at each station to aim an imaginary shotgun. She could feel the inevitable excitement building in her chest.

"A few practice shots," she said as Glenda came up to her, "and I believe I'll be all right. I hope so—I've been bragging to Ira."

"You may be safe," Glenda said wryly. "He's out of practice, as well. It's been years since I've seen him shoot. He hunted when I first knew him, but he's quit that, too."

"Why? Was he bored with it?"

"No. It was the way the game was disappearing. He talks a lot about conservation now." She laughed. "He even belongs to the Nature Conservancy. Funny place for a hunter, right?"

"I suppose so," Diane agreed and looked away, glancing again at the field as if judging it, but with her mind on Ira. Full of surprises, that man. Good surprises.

"How about Jack? Does he hunt?"

Glenda rolled her eyes. "Jack fishes. For some men that's sport; for some it's business, for Jack it's an obsession."

Diane laughed. "He's dedicated, then. I suppose that's what I want—to do something that would be important to me. Somehow, selling real estate just doesn't make it." She turned at a sound and saw the men coming down, Ira carrying a double gun case, Jack ambling along behind, his face gentling into a half smile as his eyes found Glenda.

Noting the glance, Diane thought the Griffiths seemed closer than most of the couples she had known. She was conscious of a tiny pang of envy and wondered if, deep down, she wanted that rapport with a man. Her eyes went back to Ira, swept up the bronzed, muscular legs, hesitated briefly on the snug, white shorts, passed over the lean middle and broad chest and stopped on his face, noting the sensual mouth, the hot, golden eyes that met her gaze and flared with a sudden, sexual awareness. He smiled at her, an intimate smile, and she looked away, feeling warm, realizing that she'd made him think she was remembering—or maybe dreaming about tonight. Dreaming, she thought, the only possible dream about him. Because the way he reacted confirmed what she already knew. He was exactly what she had decided he was the day they met. A wonderful lover. But he'd never confine himself to one permanent woman. Which, she reassured herself, made him exactly what she wanted.

"Vests," Jack was saying, handing the padded shooting vests to Glenda, "and goggles. Also, don't forget your ears." He grinned at Diane. "You, too. We're strict about safety."

Diane put on a vest, hung the goggles and earphones around her neck and turned to Ira, who was opening the gun case.

"Oh, beautiful! And even the stock looks right for me.... Let me hold it, Ira."

He lifted the gleaming walnut and blue steel shotgun from the case and handed it over, watching as she made sure it was empty and swung it to her shoulder, laying her cheek along the high comb of the polished stock. Even in her pleated shorts and loose, feminine blouse, even with her delicacy and the oddly childlike excitement in her eyes, he saw that she moved like an expert;

her weight on the right foot, her slender hands gripping the gun with the ease of long practice.

"So, what do you think?"

She lowered the weapon. "You know what I think. This is a treasure. What balance! You're sure you don't mind letting me use it?"

"I'm sure. Better try it out, though, with a few shots."

She was looking at him and the other gun, still in the case. She had thought Glenda was kidding when she'd said Ira shot skeet with a rifle. Those tiny disks, flying fast, twisting and turning, were hard enough to hit with an open-bore 12-gauge. If he hit even one with that 223 rifle, she'd be surprised. She looked up, seeing that he looked amused.

"If you expect a perfect score from a rifle," he said, reading the doubt in her eyes, "I'm afraid you'll be disappointed. But skeet is great for target practice."

"I can well imagine," Diane said rather stiffly. She still thought it was a grandstand play. But it was none of her business. She took the ammunition he handed her and walked toward the first station.

When he had seen Diane take her practice shots and then settle into a round, Ira chose to watch, letting Glenda and Jack handle the clay pigeons, tripping the action when Diane called.

She worked incredibly fast, calling for the next one before the echoes of her shots died away.

"Pull!" she yelled, and Jack sent a disk flying out of the high house. "Pull!" Another disk arced up from the low house, tripped by Glenda. Both Jack and Glenda whooped and laughed as the fragments of the disks blew away, yelled encouragement as Diane took the next station, set herself and called again. Ira watched, silent and thoughtful, and in the end amazed. She finished the singles round and then took a full set of doubles, when the two disks flew at once, and never missed a shot. He went down as she finished and congratulated her, seeing the iron tension behind the calm face. She removed her goggles and earphones and took a deep breath, letting it out slowly, letting the tension flow away with it.

"It wasn't all skill," she said, relaxing. "This gun is perfect. Now I'm waiting to see you handle that rifle."

He looked away. There had been too much tension there. He realized that if she said she could do something, then she felt she had to be the best at whatever it was, as if she had to live up to some impossible ideal. He answered carefully. "Not yet. I'll take over, so Glenda can shoot."

"I should have shot first," Glenda said in humorous complaint. "I've never had a perfect score in my life."

"You'd have had one often," Diane said suddenly, a tinge of bitterness in her soft voice, "if you'd been forced to live a life of nothing but practice until you did. Anyway, I'll trade skeet lessons for cooking lessons, if you'd like."

"I'd like," Glenda said promptly, and headed for the first station with her gun. "Come give me some hints."

RIDING UP to the guest house after dinner that night, Diane complained to Ira.

"You didn't shoot. I was looking forward to seeing you blast those clay birds with one little, teeny bullet."

Ira grinned. "You mean you were looking forward to seeing me miss them, don't you?"

She slumped down in the seat and stretched, laughing, closing her eyes, letting the night breeze cool her face. "Maybe. Tell me, how many have you hit with that toy?"

He gave her a sideways glance. "More than you think. Maybe I'll show you tomorrow."

She shook her head without bothering to open her eyes. "Tomorrow Glenda is teaching me how to make pot roast and apple pie." Yawning, she wriggled deeper into the seat and was quiet.

Parking behind the guest house, Ira sat for a moment in silence. "Somehow," he said finally, "I'm not sure I like all this. Giving Glenda a few pointers on skeet is all right, but you don't have to take lessons in how to cook from her." He stopped talking, his jaw snapping shut. Listening to his own voice, he had heard a note of ridiculous jealousy.

She sighed and burrowed against his shoulder, her eyes still closed. "Yes, I do. I need to learn. Besides, you have your own area of expertise as a teacher, remember?"

He looked down at her closed eyes, her sleepy face. The moonlight accented her features, casting shadows, making her black lashes look like charcoal feathers on her pale skin, making the bump in her narrow nose more obvious. Her mouth, relaxed, looked even softer. He sighed and put his arms around her, lifting her into his lap. She yawned and clung, her arm going around his neck, her cheek onto his chest.

"Is that how you think of me, Sparrow? As an expert at making love?"

Her arm tightened; her head moved affirmatively. "Mmm-hmm. World-class."

It wasn't the answer he wanted, but he had to laugh. "How would you know?"

"I know." She opened her eyes and sat up, looking at him seriously. "Anyone would. When something is perfect, you always know."

"Maybe." His throat was tight; he could feel his pulse beating there. He tried to ignore it, tried to pretend it didn't mean anything. He was too old, too wise, to believe in love, to want a lasting relationship. This would wear off. It had to. He stroked her hair and gave her what he hoped was a reassuring smile. "It takes two, Sparrow. You're a lovely, passionate woman."

Her answering smile was shaky. "With you," she said, stroking his cheek. "Only with you. Let's go in. No, let's go swimming, darling. It'll be fun! The moon is so bright...."

He started to refuse. He wanted her in his arms, in his bed, not sporting around in the moonlit surf like some teenager. Then he remembered that when she was a teenager, she had lived like a hermit and had no fun at all. "Why not?" he said, and swung her out of the Jeep, letting her slip to the ground. "All we'll need is a couple of towels and a blanket. I'll go in and get them. Wait for me on the beach."

He came down the wooden steps a few minutes later and saw her clothes heaped on the table. Looking out at the path of silver the moon laid on the smooth sea, he saw the silhouette of her head and her slim arms breaking the surface and slipping in again. Quickly he undressed and piled his clothes beside hers, flung down the blanket and towels and ran to the edge of the shore. She saw him coming and surged forward in waist-deep water, opening her arms.

"Oh, Ira, isn't this marvelous!"

He swam to her and swept her into an embrace. She was soft and cool, almost cold against his warm skin. So small and slender. But when he kissed her, the inside of her mouth was like velvet to his tongue. "Yes, marvelous. So are you."

"Am I? How?"

"The way you think simple things are marvelous. Like someone who just arrived on this planet." He kissed her again, taking his time about it. Then he held her head between his broad palms and looked into her eyes, fancying he could see their color in the bright moonlight. "Sometimes," he added huskily, "you make me feel the same. New, as if my life had just begun."

The kiss had made her dizzy again. That, and the feel of his swelling arousal against her smooth belly. She wavered with the push and tug of the waves. But Ira stood like the Rock of Gibraltar, his feet planted firmly in the yielding sand. She clung to him another moment and then made herself let go, easing down into the water again.

"My life really is new," she said with wonder. "I just realized that. Being with you has made me free." She laughed softly, reaching for his hand. "You're a great role model, darling. Free as a bird! Come on, let's swim. Maybe we'll make it to Spain this time."

"No." He loosed his hand from hers and caught her up by her wriggling waist. Pulling her with him, he waded through the waves up the beach to the blanket he'd flung onto the sand. He knelt there, easing her down onto her back, his eyes going over her hungrily, watching the rivulets of water running from her round, heaving breasts. He let out his breath in a long sigh and bent over her, looking again into her eyes. She had stopped laughing; her eyes were wide, gazing at him.

"You're more beautiful than ever, Sparrow. Why?"

Diane smiled, loving his husky tone, the intensity of his gaze, but didn't answer. She touched him instead, cupping a hand around the nape of his strong neck, urging him down, gasping as he opened his mouth and seemed to devour a breast. She fastened her fingers in his hair as heat flowed from his mouth to her chilled skin. Her own held breath shuddered out as passion pierced her like a streak of fire, running from breast to the pit of her belly. How she had wanted him, all day. She didn't want to want him, not this much.... She moved as his mouth let go, moved urgently, trying to thrust the other breast toward him, sinking back in relief when she felt him nuzzling for it, humming a growl in her throat. She was warm now, warm all over, relaxed. After a moment she loosened her hold on his hair, smoothing it back, rubbing her hands over his neck, his shoulders.

"Ira."

He raised his head and looked at her, his eyes shadowed, his nose and high cheekbones touched with silver. She smiled, trying for lightness, and pressed against his shoulders, urging him over, urging him down.

"Let me," she whispered, "let me love you." She rose and bent over him as he slowly lay back, stroking his hair out of his eyes, kissing him lightly all over his face, kissing the corners of his mouth and teasing between his lips with the point of her tongue. She touched him everywhere, moving her hands over his hard muscles, his springing body hair, feeling tension grip him, feeling the thundering beat of his heart. Her own desire rose until she ached, until she nearly cried out for him. She took his straining shaft into her hands, feeling how hot it was, how tight and smooth, smooth as stretched silk, pulsing against her palms. The ache in her breasts, the exquisite pain low in her belly, both intensified into sweet torture. She could wait no longer.

"Ira . . . oh, Ira, take me now. Please."

The arm around her tightened and drew her down. "Take me, Sparrow. I need to know you want me that much." He lifted her over him and showed her how, his big hands trembling as he pressed her down and filled her with himself. He gasped, steeling himself to wait, but Diane, feeling the heat and hardness pushing in, moved involuntarily, caught her breath with a gasp and moved again, feeling her inner flesh tighten in an irresistible spasm and then explode into waves of intense pleasure. She threw back her head and heard her own low but urgent sounds, felt his hands holding her, his body rising beneath her, thrusting and thrusting again until the ecstasy came storming back, stronger than before.

Then tears came to her eyes, tears of joy, and she leaned forward, helpless against the force of shared emotion, and laid her cheek upon his throbbing chest. His arms wrapped her tight, his hoarse sound of satisfaction rumbled in her ear. Sweet thunder after the storm.

9

IT SEEMED TO DIANE that on Eleuthera days passed like hours, weeks like days. She and Ira spent time on the yacht, taking short trips, sightseeing, being alone. Then, when she began talking of heading home, Ira put it off for a week of scuba diving with Jack and Glenda.

"We owe them a trip," Ira said, "and you'll like it. We'll go up to Harbour Island. Good diving off there."

Diane agreed. But, she thought, after this trip she was going to find something real to do. In the meantime she found a scuba school in Governor's Harbour and began to look forward to the week of diving.

They got to Harbour Island in early afternoon. They found all they needed in the first dive shop they saw, collected it and carried it from the shelves to a counter. The proprietor studied the things they laid in front of him: tanks, masks, flippers, wet suits and an underwater camera. He grinned, picking up a spear gun and pretending to aim it.

"Just pictures, no meat?"

"No meat," Ira said, glancing at Jack. "If we get fish-hungry, we've got a traditional fisherman along."

"Nice," the proprietor said, putting the spear gun down. "Some of my customers want to murder them poor fish, right in their own homes. Cruel, I call it." A man of maybe thirty or thirty-five, he was wearing a pair of old shorts and that grin, nothing else, yet seemed perfectly at ease. He picked up his own gear.

"Okay, I'm Bruce, and I'm your guide. You'll see some fish today that'll make you wish for a wide-angle lens. Come on." Going out, he grabbed the sign on his door that read Open and turned it over to Closed. "There, I don't need no more business today. Besides, I hardly ever get to dive, now that I got this damn place. Too many customers."

On board the *Sea Fever*, Bruce took over. "Evasive action," he told Ira, "until we shake the spies. Man, this is a pretty boat. I hope to hell you got a dive platform."

"We've got one," Ira said. "What kind of spies do we have to shake?"

In the other chair, Diane watched and listened. Bruce intrigued her with his raffish look and deliberate air of mystery.

Bruce watched the loran while he answered the question. "This place we're going is secret. Me and my buddies have got some real big fish, so tame they'll take food from a man's hand. Just think for a minute, friend. How long would it take a diver to clean up on grouper steaks?"

"That's right," Ira answered, frowning. "They'd swim right into a spear gun, looking for a handout."

"Right. So I ain't guiding any meat divers there. One afternoon, and I'd lose all my pets. An' now, if you don't mind, we'll turn off your loran. I don't trust nobody with the numbers on this little piece of reef."

Ira laughed and touched the loran switch. "I ran these reefs for years without loran, and I still can. Just don't ask me to turn off the depth recorder."

"Lemme take the wheel?"

Ira shook his head. "No one else runs my boat."

"Okay. Give it another ten degrees south an' keep on for a while. I'll tell you when to change directions."

Diane stood up. "Take my chair, Bruce. I've got things to do." She left, going back to the aft deck, where Jack and Glenda were. She sat, stretching her legs to the sun.

"Big deal in there," she said, amused. "Bruce made Ira turn off his loran. Maybe we're out to find buried treasure."

"If he's got what he says he's got," Jack said, "it's treasure. There aren't many big grouper left." He got up, stretching. "Guess I'll go listen to his spiel. I might learn something."

Puzzled, Diane turned to Glenda as he left. "Then it's true? The reefs are really depleted? I thought the waters around the Bahamas teemed with fish."

"They do. But it's changing fast. You know how it is—some of the divers are sports, some are spoilers. With a spear gun, a diver can make a month's income in a weekend." Glenda gave Diane an unreadable glance. "That's tempting," she added, "to people who need money. You may not understand it."

Diane swallowed and managed a smile. "Come off it, Glenda. I worked. I know how it can be."

"Maybe," Glenda said. "Maybe not. I've heard of fortunes being made in real estate. But you'd have to be a genius to make it big enough to retire at your age."

"I didn't," Diane said, fast. "A friend left me a great deal of what I have. I'm no genius." She stopped abruptly, wondering why she'd tried to explain. She felt more uncomfortable by the minute. Besides, whose business was it?

"Forget it," Glenda said, obviously reading her mind. "It's none of my business. You should have told me when I made that snide remark. I guess I'm just jealous."

"Believe me," Diane said with feeling, "no one should be jealous of my life. I've wasted a lot of years. That's why I want to change, to do something better. Some-day—"

"We're almost there," Jack said behind them. "Time to suit up."

It took nearly an hour to satisfy Bruce's requirements. He refused to allow an anchor to be set in the reef. "Set it outside, man. If it drags, set it again. The reef is alive. Don't kill it."

Ira was patient. He anchored and reanchored, using two anchors, until the chains and lengths of nylon line held. Bruce shook his head when Glenda, who disliked struggling into a wet suit, came up from below in a maillot. "Some of the coral is poisonous. A scratch will give you trouble for weeks." Glenda sighed and went back for the wet suit.

"I'm sorry I came," she told Diane. "That guy's a bore."

Diane, leaning over the side as Ira unfolded the diving platform, watched the scene below. The water was like glass, deceptively clear, looking no more than eight or ten feet deep instead of the thirty feet Ira had said it was. Coral heads in all sizes and shapes rose from the rock like sculptures, sea fans in reds and yellows and mauves waved in the drifting currents. Among the coral growths were streams of small, bright fish, brilliantly colored and oddly shaped. They swam in and out of the weed and fans, passing over patches of pink and orange sea anemones that clung to the rocks.

"Come on, Sparrow. You're going to look good down there in that yellow suit."

She straightened, smiled and let Ira help her over the stern and onto the platform as Bruce went in, surfaced long enough to adjust his mouthpiece, then slipped into a dive, swimming rapidly downward, his bag of small bait fish tied to his belt. Diane checked her equipment, turned her back to the water and let herself go. Surfacing, she saw Ira splash in beside her and laughed.

"Couldn't wait?"

"You're new at this," he pointed out, shaking his mouthpiece. "I thought you might have trouble."

"Oh." He'd been acting like a mother hen for days, being much too protective to suit her. Both Glenda and Jack had noticed, and it was a little embarrassing. Diane started to say something tart about being able to take care of herself, but bit it back. She was new at this. She smiled instead.

"Well, thanks. You're right. We can go down together."

Bruce had already tolled up the grouper. All you could see of the man was his legs. There was a wall of fish around him, black-bellied, gray grouper, weighing perhaps thirty-five pounds; and huge, dark warsaws, moving with sluggish dignity, that would go well over a hundred. As Jack and Glenda came down, the big bodies moved aside and Bruce came swimming out, bringing the rest of his bait, dividing it among the reaching hands. In minutes the fish were back, the bait was in their cavernous mouths, and they had begun slowly drifting away to the shadowed lee of the bigger rocks. Now the divers began to enjoy the sights of a truly pristine reef. As Bruce had promised, there was no damage here, no sign of man's interference.

This was Diane's first experience with any reef, and she was fascinated. There was something alive, something odd, something beautiful or something weird either growing on every inch of the reef or swimming over it. She went from point to point, hovering to look, weaving on and stopping again, moving her flippers just enough to keep the current from pushing her away. She kept turning her head to catch Ira's eyes, smile and point and swim on again. Once when she looked back, she saw he had taken the camera from his belt and was taking her picture. She waved him away and swam on.

Ira followed, watching her. She reminded him of a bee in a field of summer clover, drunk with nectar but unable to resist the blooms ahead. They were getting farther and farther away from Bruce and the Griffiths, closer and closer to the edge of the reef and the steep drop to the ocean floor. He stopped idling and caught up with her, grasping her arm and pointing back when she looked around.

She shook her head, pointing the other way to a forest of ghostly white sea fans against a moss-covered, emerald rock. A school of silver angelfish with blue stripes and trailing fins was swimming above the fans.

He nodded and went with her, slowing to let her watch. Then, in the blink of an eye, the fish disappeared, dropping like stones into the fans. Puzzled, Diane spread her hands questioningly.

Ira's head swung, staring along the suddenly empty reef. Jack and Glenda were swimming up to the boat, fast. All the fish had vanished. In the distance Bruce motioned sharply for them to come back, and Ira pushed Diane that way, pointing at the gesturing Bruce, nodding for her to go. She went, startled by the change in the reef, feeling wary without knowing why, and glad when she felt Ira brush against her and knew he was following. Then, just as she decided it was nothing to worry about, Ira grabbed her and pushed her down behind a projecting coral head. Settling beside her, hunching his broad shoulders and chest over her, throwing a leg over her thighs, he pointed to the edge of the reef and up to where the clear water was darkened, as if by a cloud.

She saw the fish and felt the vibration through the water at the same time. There were hundreds, no, thousands of them. Thick-bodied, streamlined, dark, silvergray fish with huge, wild-looking eyes, traveling so close together they blocked out the light from the sky. They were passing so rapidly they blurred into a solid mass...a terrified mass! That knowledge came to her instinctively, and chilled her to the bone. Ira knew. That was why he had pushed her down, why he had hidden her as well as he could beneath his own body. Those fish were racing away from danger—a danger that could also threaten Ira and herself.

Diane watched, forcing herself to breathe slowly, evenly. She could feel the tension in Ira, see it in the line of his jaw. Then came a sudden tumult in the midst of the fish; they scattered and came back together in a jostling, frantic crush, racing on. Another flashing, foaming collision began and fish leaped, darted aside or dropped, gushing blood, quivering, spiraling slowly down. Out of the mass above a long, gray torpedo shape came shooting down, turned on one side, opened a mouth bristling with teeth and took a fish. Sharks! Sharks herding a huge school of fish like sheep, killing and eating. A silent scream burst in Diane's head, she felt her body convulse, trying to get away. Ira's grip on her became a steel band; his weight held her down, his thigh clamped her thrashing legs. She twisted and looked through his mask, seeing his tiger eyes intense, demanding obedience. Then she realized he was right; a frantic, fleeing body would just bring the sharks.

In fear and horror she watched as the fish leaped and bled and died. The water turned murky with blood, pieces of bleeding flesh rained down, the sharks wove through a reddened curtain of death in a feeding frenzy, chopping at anything that moved. On the reef nothing stirred, though occasionally the sharks would swing in and pass over the rocks, their small eyes gleaming, alert. At these times Diane stared down, seeing nothing but Ira's hand gripping her arm. She felt cold, cold as death as the shadows passed over them.

At last it was over. The fish had moved on, the sharks had followed. Ira took his weight from her and stood, helping her up. He questioned her with his eyes, laid a hand upon the valve that would switch her oxygen tanks and raised his brows. She nodded, needing new energy, then pointed at the long shadow of the *Sea Fever* above them to the north. Behind his mask, Ira's eyes warmed to her, and he nodded emphatically, motioning her up. Bruce was already on his way; he waited for them at the diving platform and helped them on, grinning, mouthpiece and mask dangling on his chest. On deck they divested themselves of the tanks, the masks, the flippers. Bruce followed them into the saloon, talking.

"Damn good thing you knew enough to get down, Nicholson. Even I couldn't make it to the boat in time. But you got to admit it was a damn good show. You don't see something like that every day, man."

"Once is enough," Ira said, his eyes on Diane. She was pale, her eyes strained, her soft mouth tremulous. She looked exhausted. "Come on," he said, "you need a hot shower and a rest."

"I'll help her," Glenda said quickly, coming up the companionway. She was dry, dressed in slacks and a shirt, but her pleasant face was nearly as pale as Diane's. Ira smiled and shook his head.

"I need a shower myself. Rustle up some snacks, Glenda, and make some coffee. We'll be back."

Silent, Diane preceded him down to the staterooms. In the bath she took off the wet suit and the bikini she wore under it, and waited while Ira adjusted the shower, standing there like a shamed child. When he reached for her to bring her under the warm spray, she looked up at him with tears in her eyes.

"I was terrified," she burst out. "If you hadn't held me down I would've been eaten! Chopped all up like those poor fish. Oh, God! I'm a coward, Ira. And stupid. A stupid c-c-coward. My father was right. I'm no damn good."

He let her cry, her hot tears washing away with the salt from the sea. He washed her hair along with his own, rinsed it squeaky clean, and when she stopped sobbing and crying he washed her face, kissed her gently and turned off the shower.

"Now, listen," he said, handing her a towel. "The only difference between us down there was experience. I knew what to do, you didn't. So I did it for both of us. But I don't think I've been that scared since I was a kid. When those big devils cruised in over our heads, I thought I'd have a heart attack."

She stared at him, her reddened eyes full of hope. "You aren't just saying that?"

"Hell, no! I mean every word. You were great, Sparrow. I was afraid you'd keep on struggling, but you conquered your fear like a veteran. Believe me, your father was wrong. You won that battle. There wasn't another peep out of you."

She let out her breath with a big sigh and moved into his arms, hugging him. "I was too scared to peep," she said, "But . . . thank you. I feel better, a lot better." She moved away, catching up a terry robe and rubbing her hair with the towel, looking for the blower to dry it.

Putting on the robe, she thought how well he always understood everything, how much he knew about making a woman feel wonderful. All the time. About anything. She glanced back at him. He was half-dressed, his white shorts on, his head emerging from a yellow pullover, damp hair tousled, his broad mouth nearly grim, as if he was still remembering the sharks, the killing, his eyes dark and thoughtful as he met her gaze.

"Want me to bring you something to eat? A cup of coffee?"

"No, thanks." She found the blower and sat down to use it. "I'll be up in a few minutes." She smiled at him as he left, a dazzling, grateful smile. He really was perfect, or close to perfect. He looked fantastic; he made wonderful love; he had a kind and generous nature. He had known exactly what to say and how to say it to bring her confidence back, to make her feel whole again. Staring into the mirror, she thought about what he had said earlier. *The only difference between us down there was experience.*

She sighed. The main difference between them up here was experience, too. Ira Nicholson knew a lot more about women than she knew about men. But she did know one thing. She had picked a winner. He was exactly what she needed, all she needed. And that wasn't a guess or an opinion. He had shown her she had a healthy sexual response, he had let her know that he, an experienced man, was attracted to her, and loved making love with her. And it wasn't because she was Harrington Roberts's daughter and heiress. Some men might plan all this and then come up with a marriage proposal after they figured she trusted them, but not Ira. That was the good part. That was the part that made everything else believable. He had told her up front—the first time they'd talked, really—that even the idea of marriage terrified him. It terrified her, too. Didn't it?

She frowned a little and put down the brush, thinking. Of course it did. She had to remember that. Marriage for her was out of the question. Because, she thought wryly, while there were at least a billion reasons why a man would propose if she gave him a chance, none of them was because of her. They were all neatly tucked away in Harrington Roberts's investments.

10

THEY WENT BACK to the same reef the next day; because, Ira said, they had a memory of defeat. Going down, Diane clenched her teeth on her mouthpiece to keep them from chattering, but she went. Glenda refused.

They fed the big grouper and explored, took dozens of underwater pictures, returned Bruce to Harbour Island in time to make it back home themselves. The seas were calm, and Jack and Glenda stayed on the aft deck, lounging in comfort. Diane joined Ira in the wheelhouse, grateful for the privacy.

"We'll spend another day at Governor's Harbour," Ira said after a while, "and then move on." He sounded as if he meant to keep his reasons hidden, and Diane didn't argue.

"Where will we go? Back to Miami?"

He glanced at her quickly. "Only if you insist."

She smiled faintly. "I should, but I don't want to."

"Good. We'll head down toward the Exumas and see what we find. I'd like more time alone with you." He wondered why he'd said that last and what she would think of it. It was true, of course, but he wished it weren't. His life had been simple and easy before he met this woman, and it was beginning to irritate him that now, looking back at the way it was, it seemed empty and lacking in warmth. Lonely. But lonely or not, he didn't want any of the complications that went with permanent relationships. Then neither did she, so why worry?

He looked over at her and smiled, the first real smile he'd managed since the sharks came the day before. "That is," he added, "if you don't mind."

"You know I don't mind. I like exploring new places, and I've never been to the Exumas. What are they like?"

"To the cruising yachts, they're like a string of green pearls, running south between Eleuthera and Andros Islands." He smiled. "You'll see. I'd still rather show than tell."

They were back at Governor's Harbour before dark. Driving to the house, Ira filled in Jack and Glenda.

"So," he concluded, "I'll need to get a few supplies. If you'll bring Diane and the bags down, we can leave at noon."

"There goes my skeet partner," Glenda moaned. "Just when I started getting in shape. Bring her back again, Ira."

"I'll try. What idiot is back there, blowing a horn?"

Glenda craned to look, then burst into unrestrained laughter. "Edie," she said when she could, "Edie Laurant! Sure you don't want to leave right now, Ira?"

Ira groaned. "One more day and I wouldn't have been here. Is she alone?"

"No. There's a man—looks like Don Mueller. We'll have to ask them to dinner." She turned to Diane. "Hey! Don't look so negative. They can be amusing at times. But brace yourself. Edie makes a big play for Ira every time she sees him."

"I know her," Diane said stiffly. "I know Don, too."

"You do?" Glenda was surprised. "I wouldn't have thought you ran in that crowd. All they do is party and bed hop."

"I didn't run with them," Diane said, stung. "I know them through other people." She felt Ira's glance.

"Through Paul," she added to them. "Paul thinks Don is wonderful."

Ira gave a short nod, slowing for the turn into the lot near the big house. "We're leaving tomorrow," he reminded her quietly, "I guess we can take one evening. Don will probably be hiring Jack as a mate on his sportfishing cruiser. We don't want to queer Jack's deal."

Edie Laurant hadn't changed, Diane thought. Her hair was still a brilliant red gold and fashionably tousled, her figure, contained in a sleeveless, and nearly backless, beige silk jumpsuit was still lush with curves, her greenish eyes wide and her smile delighted. She rushed forward, flung herself into Ira's arms and pulled his head down for a kiss.

"Ira, darling! What a marvelous coincidence! I haven't seen you for ages. You remember Don, don't you?"

"Yes, of course." Ira pulled away from her clutching arms, shook hands with Mueller and looked around for Diane. She came forward.

"Hello, Edie," she said, stepping around her, "it's been a long time, hasn't it?"

Edie jumped and whirled. "Why... my God, it's Diane Roberts! What in the h—world are you doing here?"

Glenda stepped in, fast. "She's here with Ira, Edie. Don, do you know Diane?"

"I certainly do," Don said and came to take Diane's hand. A thin, nervous man with graying hair, he seemed anxious to smooth over the awkward moment. He stood talking a moment, saying how long it had been since he'd seen Paul. "And even longer since I've seen you," he added. "So strange to find you here—but then, it's a small world."

"A crazy world," Edie said, recovering her poise. "Full of crazy people. You never know what anyone's going to do. Shall we bring our bags in, Glenda, or are the rooms full?"

"Plenty of room," Glenda said smoothly. "Ira and Diane are in the cottage. Let Jack help you with those bags, Don."

As the two men went to the trunk of Edie's car, Edie swung around to the others again, her narrowed eyes going to Diane's face. "I'm sorry Diane—I forgot to offer my sympathy for your recent loss. After such a close relationship, I'm sure you must miss old Yuri Stephan."

"Yes," Diane said. "I do. Very much."

Edie's eyes widened. "Really? Then I suppose you were forced by grief to get away and forget—with a much more attractive man." She stopped, seeming breathless at her daring. "Or was it to stay out of Paul's way for a while? It seems he thinks he can prove old Yuri was under undue influence, when he signed over the family home and business to you."

Glenda drew in her breath, looking helplessly from Edie to Diane, but Ira moved forward between them. "Edie," he said harshly, "you're making a fool of yourself. Shut up." He saw Diane's face was white with fatigue and pain.

"It's all right," Diane told him, touching his arm. "She's Paul's friend, and not mine. Let's go in, Ira. I want to bathe and dress before dinner."

"But do come back here," Glenda said quickly. "I've casseroles in the freezer that will feed us all."

"We'll go into town," Ira said flatly, "and eat in peace. We'll see you and Jack tomorrow."

"Oh, don't be so touchy, Ira," Edie said, clutching at him. "I was only repeating what I'd heard." She glanced at Diane. "You didn't mind, did you? If you did, I'm sorry."

Diane met the greenish eyes. "I mind rudeness, Edie. But what you said about Paul is true. He does feel that way."

Edie smiled triumphantly. "Then you'll come back and eat with us?"

Ira shook Edie's hand loose and took Diane's arm. "She'll eat with me," he said, "at Raleigh's Inn." He looked past Edie at Glenda. "Tell Jack I'll pick him up in the morning, so he can bring the Jeep back."

They were halfway to the guest house before Ira spoke again. "We'll pack together," he said, "before we go to bed. You'll come with me in the morning, and when we're ready to leave, we'll leave. I'll be damned if Edie's going to get another chance to claw you to shreds."

"We have things at both houses," Diane pointed out. "But I don't mind if Edie's around. She's not important to me."

"She hurt you. I could see it in your eyes."

"Only because she insulted Yuri with her stupid remarks. I don't care what she thinks of me." She smiled as she saw his doubtful glance. "I truly don't, Ira. Edie isn't worth worrying about."

Turning in toward the small house, Ira slowed and hunched his tense shoulders, dropping them to relax. "Okay. I believe you. But I'm still not letting her use you as a target. I care, whether you do or not."

THE BAR and small dining room of Raleigh's Inn had begun life as the superstructure of an old, but magnificent yacht. Behind the bar were the huge wheel and binnacle, all polished mahogany and brass. The dining room was the main saloon, the aft cabin had been made into private dining niches, and each space had beautifully fitted and curved walls, hanging ships' lanterns of brass and

heavy tables and chairs made of rock maple and upholstered with leather. A place of shadows and warm,
glowing light, a place to sit and look into someone's eyes,
a place to dream.

"I know a spot on one of the Exuma cays that will suit
us," Ira said over after-dinner brandy. "There are a few
cabins there, right on the beach, but secluded from each
other. There's a well of fresh water and a dock." He
smiled, his eyes gleaming golden in the warm light. "No
telephones," he added, "except at a tiny yacht club. And
no one we know lives there."

Diane's gaze was faraway, dreaming and soft. "Is there
such a place? They say you can go to the ends of the earth
and meet an acquaintance by accident."

"On Norman's Cay," Ira said, sounding amused, "the
acquaintance would pretend he didn't see you."

Diane sat up, staring at him. "Norman's Cay? Isn't that
where the man who claimed to be the king of a Colom-
bian cocaine cartel set up his kingdom?"

Ira laughed. "In a manner of speaking, yes. But the
Bahamian government ran him off some years ago, after he had spent millions acquiring the land. He trashed
the place before he left, burned the buildings and left in
a high-speed boat to avoid capture. The island has managed to ease back into its usual, slow and comfortable
pace, and the former residents have returned."

"Then there's no danger?"

"Not here. Not in the main Bahamian islands. Only
between the Inaguas and Puerto Rico, where yachts are
warned either to travel in groups or to be sure they can
outrun the smugglers."

She looked at him curiously. "What would a smuggler want with a slow yacht?"

"Money," Ira said. "Food, water, provisions and fuel. Waiting for a calm night and a fast run to Florida, they run out of things." He paused, his jaw tensing. "I lost some friends that way. A couple, in an old, slow trawler they'd made into a home. Burned pieces of the boat were found, with bullet holes sprayed in the wood, but that was all."

"That's horrible. Killing innocent people for food and fuel and spending money! They're like pirates."

Ira nodded, rising and pulling out her chair. "They are pirates. Men join for the money and thrill of running drugs, but once they're in, they do as they're told. Arguing with one of those captains is suicide."

Diane tried to take it in. "It seems impossible," she said, leaving the table. "Murder in vacation heaven. What about the authorities? Can't they do something?"

"Sure. If they can find them. Sometimes they do. But even with radio communication, it's a hell of a lot of water to cover." He took her arm and stepped outside, heading for the Jeep. "But don't worry, we aren't going that way."

"Good." She yawned, then yawned again and laughed, leaning against his shoulder. "Sorry about that. It's been a long day."

"Too long." Ira helped her into the Jeep. Climbing in, he put an arm around her and pulled her close. "I'm sorry, Sparrow. I've been pushing all day. After the dive we should have stayed there and come home tomorrow—but I couldn't wait. I like the Griffiths, but I'm tired of having them around all the time. I want you to myself."

"I know. I feel the same." She yawned once more, her face pressed against his neck, then touched her tongue to his skin, tasting the warm, salty flavor that was all his. "Mmm, that's good. Let's go to bed."

He laughed and started the Jeep. "Best offer I've had today. I'll take it."

At the guest house they made sweet, lazy love, sighing, suddenly hot love, in a black and moonless night. They saw each other only with their hands, tracing the features of a face, the shape of a breast, the length and breadth of a muscled back. Ira whispered his question again.

"Why does this keep getting better?"

"Because you make such lovely love."

"That can't be true. I haven't changed." *Oh, yes, you have. You've never been in love before.*

"But I have," she answered, "oh, I have, darling. And I know why."

IN THE MORNING they threw their belongings together and left, riding down to the big house in sleepy silence. Stopping the Jeep, Ira jumped out and turned.

"Anything else here but the guns?"

Diane looked at him in surprise. "I'm not sure. I'll look around."

"You don't have to come in, Sparrow."

"Yes, I do. I want to thank Glenda and Jack for their hospitality to me. Besides..." she slipped out and smiled, taking his arm "...I don't run from people like Edie Laurant."

Glenda met them at the door and insisted on making coffee and providing fruit and rolls. "Jack is up, too," she said, "but no one else. He'll help you carry things out, Ira, while Diane and I put the coffee on."

In the kitchen Diane made coffee while Glenda, who seemed tense and on edge, got out the fruit and heated the rolls.

"Edie told me who you were," Glenda said abruptly. "No wonder you said you didn't need money. Your father—"

"My father," Diane interrupted in a flash of anger, "doesn't give me a cent and won't, unless I live with him and do as he tells me. And I'm not going to do that. What I have I made myself, except for what Yuri Stephan gave me."

"Edie told me about that, too," Glenda said, avoiding her gaze. "And well, I figure that's none of my business. But she did say you were going to get a shock when you got back to Miami. I thought I'd better tell you that part."

"Well, thanks," Diane said wryly. "I guess I can wait." Setting out mugs and spoons on the kitchen bar, she studied Glenda's averted face. "I worked with Yuri," she said finally, "for years. When he became too ill to handle the corporation, I took it over, and I lived in his house and took care of him. He was a wonderfully kind and intelligent old man, and I loved him very much, but he was never my lover. Does that help?"

Glenda turned sharply and stared at her. "It sure does. Edie made it sound like you took advantage of an old, foolish man." She came over and put her arms around Diane. "I'm sorry I even listened. I should have known better."

Diane hugged her back. "A lot of people who didn't know us well have thought that, Glenda. I suppose Edie thinks it's true. Anyway, I'm glad you don't."

Letting her go, Glenda smiled suddenly. "Edie does believe it, I'm sure. She also sounded as if she wished she'd thought of it first."

They were laughing when Ira and Jack came in and sat with them. "Nice sound," Ira said, looking from one to the other. "Something funny?"

"One of those things you can't explain," Diane answered. "Have some coffee."

A half hour later Ira and Diane headed for the parking lot and the Jeep. Jack came with them to bring the Jeep back and Glenda tagged along to say goodbye. They had reached the end of the roofed walkway, when Edie's voice came from an open window above them.

"Well, I'm willing to bet Ira is running out of money at last, whether you think so or not! Why else would he be making a play for Harrington Roberts's skinny daughter?"

Don's reply was only an angry mumble.

Below, the four looked at each other, grimaced and went on. Getting into the Jeep, Ira turned to Glenda. "Tell Edie that my financial status is in fine shape, and my choice of companions considerably better in every way than Don's."

Glenda laughed. "I will. In private, though. Don would feel awful. Oh, well, we all know Edie gets vicious when she's outclassed. Goodbye, you two. Have fun!"

Jack took them out to the *Sea Fever*, handed up the bags, boxes and guns and asked where they were heading.

Ira hesitated. "I suppose someone ought to know," he said finally, "in case of emergency. But remember, we won't be looking for company. I plan to take a place on Norman's Cay. You can reach me there through the little club."

Jack grinned. "Got it. Emergencies only."

"Right."

Carrying her baggage into the saloon, Diane felt her spirits rising like bubbles in champagne. This was what she wanted more than anything else—to be alone with Ira. It was wonderful that he felt the same. She clattered down the steps, stowed the baggage in the first stateroom she came to and ran back up, hearing the diesels turn over with a roar and thump, hearing the winch whine as the anchor rope tightened and then began to come in, dragging up the length of chain and anchor.

Turning at the galley level, she went forward into the wheelhouse and slid into the chair opposite Ira's. The engines were settling in, the roaring cough changing to a rumble as Ira moved the throttle ahead. Once on their way, she could see Ira's tension easing, his big body relaxing into the padded chair. He looked at her, his flat cheeks creased with his grin, his strange eyes softening into playful warmth.

"About time we got away," he said. "But I should warn you, you're going to fall in love with this next place."

Watching his eyes touch her, move slowly over her face, Diane was seized by a feeling of premonition. Now that the adventure was almost over, maybe she'd be dumb enough to fall in love with him, too. *Idiot*, she thought half angrily. *Can't you control yourself?* Her chin lifted. "I hope not. That would be a very short affair."

His smile broadened and he turned away, watching the channel ahead. "Maybe," he conceded, still playful, "and maybe not. Neither of us have any immediate plans for the future."

She laughed a little and slid out of her chair. "I do. I'm going to put things away. How much time do I have?"

"Plenty. We'll drop down to the end of Eleuthera today, get fuel and spend the night aboard. Then we'll have a reasonably straight shot across Exuma Sound that will put us in Norman's Cay tomorrow afternoon. Weather permitting."

"Fine. Oh . . . where do I put the guns?"

"In a drawer under the couch in the saloon," Ira said absently, his eyes busy with a cruiser cutting across his path. "There's a handle at the aft end. Just twist it."

She nodded and left, going into the saloon and sorting through the bags and boxes, laying the gun case on the couch, putting Ira's suitcase at the companionway steps and carrying the groceries into the galley.

She now knew where everything went. It gave her a sense of domestic efficiency to move back and forth in the galley, putting the bread into its box, wines in their gimbaled rack, the fruit in its heavy basket, the butter and cheese and eggs and meat on their various refrigerator shelves. Finished, she folded and stowed the paper bags and went into the saloon.

The polished wood beneath the couch did not look like a drawer. For one thing it had no handles. Then she remembered Ira had said the handle was on the aft end and she was to twist it. She went to the end and looked, seeing a large knob carved like a rosette protruding from the wood. She twisted it, moving out of the way as the underneath part of the couch quietly slid out onto the rug. She looked into the sliding drawer and her eyes widened. Then she straightened and marched back into the wheelhouse.

"Are we going to declare war on someone?"

Ira looked up, startled, then laughed. "I told you, I carry samples. I know it looks like an arsenal, but I like having them aboard. Those infrared scopes on the military rifles are my main stock-in-trade. I hold the patent."

"Oh. You invented the night scope?"

"Not the first one. But this improved version is mine."

"Wonderful! Does it really help you see in the dark?"

He smiled. "'Help' is the operative word. It finds what light there is—star shine, reflections from clouds, any light, no matter how faint—and concentrates it, showing you the target. But if you tried to use the night scope inside a cave, where there is no light, it wouldn't work at all."

Diane's eyes gleamed. "I want to try it. Could I?"

"Why not?" He sounded amused." We'll set up a target someday—or should I say some night?—and let you play."

She punched his shoulder with a fist. "Don't laugh at me, you rat. I can do it. You'll see." She left, going back to look again at the gleaming row of weapons, the automatic rifles, the short arms, automatic and semiautomatic. She tucked the case of skeet guns into the space allotted for it and slid the drawer back in. It went in with ease, rolling on bearings and catching on an inside mechanism controlled by the wooden rosette. Carefully planned, she thought, and why not? It was his lifework. His business. She discovered she was pleased by the fact that he'd made his own fortune, and had done it in such an imaginative and unusual way.

By evening they were anchored in the lee of Rainey's Point, which, Ira said, was directly across Exuma Sound from Norman's Cay. Their fuel tanks had been filled at a small, but choice marina, located on the south end of Eleuthera's coast, and they were completely alone. No other boat was within sight. In shorts and a skimpy, silk top, Diane leaned on the rail near the stern and watched a handful of tiny, bright yellow- and black-striped fish play in the swirl of tide running under the boat. Beneath them the rays of light from the evening sky dropped down and down, silver spears in water as clear as a blue diamond.

"Thunderstorm weather," Ira said behind her, bringing out predinner drinks in plastic glasses. "I'm glad I set two anchors again. There's wind in that squall to the northwest."

Diane came to him, taking a glass. "A breeze would be welcome." She reached up and ran her fingers along his upper lip, wiping away the beads of perspiration. "See? It's June, you know. Miserable in Miami, and not too great here, either."

"Alaska," Ira said and sat down in a deck chair. "Next June we'll be in Alaska. How does that sound?"

"Cooler. What would we be doing?" She pulled a chair over and sat with him, her back to the wind.

"I happen to know," Ira answered, "what *I* would be doing. I've been offered a job up there in a proposed national park, studying the habitat of Alaskan wildlife." He looked over at her and smiled. "There are still openings in the group. No salary, by the way, if you decide to join in."

Her face turned to the suddenly freshening wind, Diane remembered what Glenda had said. "Part of your work for conservation, I suppose. I'd be useless—I'm not qualified."

He took her hand, holding it loosely between the chairs. "I'm qualified enough for two," he said. "I'll teach you."

She laughed and turned toward him again, seeing him glance past her and suddenly get to his feet. "You're not fair, Ira. Bragging is my field. . . ." Her hands flew to her long hair as a gust caught it and sent it streaming past her face. "Good heavens, feel that wind!" She saw Ira was grabbing his chair and reaching for her, so she leaped up, got her chair and went with him toward the saloon. The rain came, making them gasp at the stinging fusillade of big, wind-driven drops that soaked them through. The boat swung, bucked against the rising waves and settled once more.

"Now that..." The rest of what Ira was saying was lost in a resounding crash of thunder that shook the boat. He looked at Diane's wide eyes and drew her into his arms.

"Never mind, Sparrow. We're safe here, and a squall won't last long." The air conditioning made their wet clothes icy, but the heat from their bodies, the feel of her warm breasts under wet silk was strangely exciting. He pulled her closer, so her small, hard nipples pressed into him, and felt himself grow hard in reaction. Thunder rolled again farther away, as Diane laughed and slid her arms around his neck.

"Think," she murmured, "think of warm, pulsing water touching us instead of these cold, wet clothes. Think of that bath oil with the marvelous fragrance. Think of our hands, smoothing it over each other...."

"Yes," he said against her lips, "yes and yes." Following her down to the stateroom and Jacuzzi, shivering in the cold air and with anticipation, Ira put his arms around her as they reached the corridor, closing his hands over her breasts, walking with her so her rounded hips swayed entrancingly against him. "Explain to me," he whispered into one ear, "how my frigid little Sparrow became such a wonderful lover."

Murmurous laughter hummed in her throat. "Once more," she said, reaching for the door to the stateroom, "the only difference between us was experience." She turned in his arms as they went in and kissed him, her tongue teasing expertly. Then she was moving away, breathless, stripping her clothes off and turning to meet his hot, golden gaze. "Thanks to you," she said softly, "the difference is gone."

11

AT NOON THE NEXT DAY the *Sea Fever* eased through islands that were little more than sandbars and came slowly into the harbor at Norman's Cay. At first, the only signs of life Diane could see were three large sailboats anchored out a way from the land and seemingly empty.

The cay itself was small. Flat, except for a few, towering, Australian pines, a good many palms, sea grapes and bay trees, with underbrush crowding some and others growing on plain sand. Diane spotted a few houses that were nearly hidden in the trees.

She studied the shore. There seemed to be some commercial development on a broad point of land that protruded from the widest section of the cay. There was a large dock there and, farther in, what looked like a small clubhouse. In both directions from that point were inviting beaches, white scallops of sand against the always beautifully blue water.

"Around the tip of the island to your left," Ira said, "the trees come down closer to the shore, so you have shade to sit in on the beach. That's where we'll look for a place to stay."

"Fine," Diane said, aware that she sounded slightly uncertain. "Wonderful, maybe. On the other hand, there's nothing wrong with staying aboard."

"It's not private enough if we stay at the dock, and too confining if we anchor out," Ira said. "It's a bother to row back and forth."

She gazed at him, surprised. He was, she thought, simply making excuses. "All right. If you want to go to the trouble of moving everything off and on again for only a week."

He glanced at her quickly and then away, slowing as they approached the long dock. "We could stay longer."

She stared at the side of his averted face, the line of flat, bronzed cheek, the heavy, dark brow, the corner of his broad mouth. All of it looked stubborn. This was something she hadn't expected and didn't know how to handle. She had thought in the beginning that he might get bored or impatient with her; she had wondered if she might have to make up a reason for cutting the cruise short. It had never crossed her mind that he might want to extend it. Besides, surely he knew—as she knew instinctively—that it was time to end this affair? They had reached a point where it seemed necessary either to say goodbye or move into a deepening relationship, which was something neither of them had ever wanted.

"It's been a wonderful time," she said gently. "And a week more is a lovely bonus. But it's time we both got back into our real worlds."

The *Sea Fever* slid along the dock and stopped. Cutting off the engines, Ira stepped outside and grabbed a line, securing the boat to a cleat on the dock. Then he stepped back in and faced her.

"Our real worlds, Sparrow? You and I are real together."

Diane was reminded of the first day they'd met, in the Biscay Yacht Basin. Today he was wearing only a pair of old, faded shorts, like the ones he had worn then. And he was still blatantly, beautifully male. Bronzed, gleaming with health, his carved, sensual mouth softening as he studied her, the look in his golden eyes burning her, demanding an answer. She couldn't deny him the truth.

"Yes, we're real. Maybe too real." She smiled and slid from the seat, picking up two used, plastic glasses and carrying them through to the galley. "And you're right, of course. This last week must be the best. Go find the cabin you want, and I'll clean up a bit here and pack our clothes and food. . . ." She stopped as Ira crowded her against a cabinet, gasped as he buried his fingers in her shining hair and kissed her, long and passionately. When he took his mouth from hers, they still clung to each other, pressed together full length.

His mouth touched her ear as he whispered, "The last week, Sparrow? I don't want to believe that."

Neither did she. Not then, with his aroused body against her, his arms around her. But there was one cold, frightened spot in her mind that drew back. She was much too close to danger, trembling on the edge of loving him. She knew if she fell, it would be all the way, and then this man, who would never break her bones or scar her face, would hurt her worse than Ben Clifton ever had. He would break her heart.

She tried to answer casually. "Who knows, darling? We may get together again."

He leaned back and looked at her in disbelief, searching her face. "Are you telling me it's over for you?"

She could suddenly feel the heat of tears coming up into her eyes. She looked down, concentrating on the sun-bleached, springing hair on his chest. "No. But it's time, Ira."

"I see." His deep voice was harsh as he let her go and turned away. "I remember now. This is an adventure, and when it's over, it's over. And somehow we're supposed to know when that happens. But—what if we can't agree?"

She shook her head, her throat too tight to answer. Ira threw up his hands and stalked away, going out to secure the rest of the lines to the dock. In a few minutes he was back, standing in the opening to the saloon.

"I'm going ashore to look for a place to stay." He hesitated for a moment and then added, "For a week."

Drying the washed glasses, Diane managed a smile. "All right. I'll be ready." *As ready as I'll ever be*, she thought, *and on guard*. Ira Nicholson was a potent adversary.

He was back in an hour, driving a homemade vehicle with a funny little wooden booth to sit in, a planked section behind for carrying luggage, and not much else but an engine and a set of enormous tires. He parked and came out toward the pile of bags and the boxes of food she'd put out for the move.

Diane stepped onto the dock with the last of the bags and spoke tentatively. "Some taxi."

Ira grinned, no longer upset. "That's an official beach buggy and I've rented it. It's ideal—never gets stuck. I've rented a place, too. I think Robinson Crusoe designed it."

Diane was relieved by his cheerful humor. "I'll accept that. It sounds appropriate."

Once loaded, the baggage and boxes of food and wine made an impressive mound on the buggy's rear platform. The first hint of trouble came when she watched Ira tie everything down with a spiderweb of rope. He grinned when he saw her staring.

"That will keep it from bouncing off. Did I say we're going primitive?"

She lifted her chin and looked down her nose at him. "Is that the same as going native?"

"Hell, no. The natives here are civilized." He gave her such a bland and innocent look that she had to laugh.

"Okay. Now I'm curious." She climbed into the little booth and sat rather gingerly on the cracked leather seat. The thing looked clean enough, though the floor was an inch deep in sand. It swayed alarmingly as Ira got in, but she clutched the post that held the homemade windshield and stayed where she was, hearing him chuckle.

"Spoilsport. You were supposed to land in my lap. Ready?"

"Yes, of course."

She regretted the remark almost immediately. The buggy roared into action. Rounding the curve to the left, it tore along the uneven, slanting beach in leaps and bounds, terrifying her at first. Then, as she realized the huge, soft tires absorbed all the shocks, she began to laugh, looking over at Ira while clinging to her post and bracing her feet.

"It's fun!"

His laugh rang out. "Sure it is. It's like a carnival ride. Remember those wild cars that bounced off each other?"

Still laughing, she shook her head. "I wasn't allowed to go to carnivals. But if they were anything like this, I would have loved it."

He put on the brakes and slewed sideways to a rocking stop. "Want to drive?"

"Oh, yes!" She scrambled out and ran around, heels sinking into the soft sand. "Is there anything I need to know?"

He got out, helped her in and went around to take her place. "The main thing is that if you turn, you make it slow and wide. The rest of it is easy."

"Turns," she repeated breathlessly, "slow and wide. Okay—you ready?"

He nodded and began to laugh helplessly as she shot forward and leaped a small dune. She looked like a child, red with excitement, her eyes blazing. She gripped the wheel and headed for another bump. "Hang on, Ira! Hang on!"

"Don't worry," he managed through his laughter, "I will. Try to miss that driftwood."

She swerved around the chunk of wood with a magnificent, airborne hop, whooped and gunned the engine, flying down the empty beach. He let her go past the place they should have turned, let her play at hopscotch until they could see people wandering on the beach in the distance. Then she slowed and stopped, catching her breath, looking at him with dazed pleasure.

"I don't want to frighten anyone," she said. "Let's switch sides again. You take us the rest of the way."

Passing him at the back of the buggy, she flung her arms around him and hugged him hard. "Thank you," she said, "for taking me to the carnival."

"You're welcome," he answered gravely. "I'm always ready to do my best for a deprived child."

He drove back slowly to a turn that took them up into a thick growth of bay and palms and turned even more slowly for the trip in, giving her plenty of time to look. She looked and grew silent.

Inside the trees was a space cleared of underbrush and holding a hut. The hut had a thatched roof, walls of driftwood that came halfway up from the ground and turned into large, screened windows.

Ira stopped the beach buggy and Diane got out, going to the screened windows to peer inside. A double bed, a couple of chairs and a lamp; wide shelves, holding sheets and towels. She continued around the hut. In the back was a roofed, open-air space with an ancient refrigerator that ran on bottled gas and a stove to match. There was a table with four chairs, a chest and a sink with a faucet. She turned the faucet and water gushed out. She looked at Ira.

"Where's the bathroom?"

He pointed and she followed with her eyes. A pipe ran up the side of a palm and curved, holding a shower head. Past that, nearly hidden among the trees, was a small wooden building with a crescent moon cut in the door.

"Primitive is right! Is this some kind of a joke?"

"No. Don't you like to camp out?"

"How would I know? I've never tried it."

"Then this is your chance." He led the way back to the buggy and began untying the nylon rope. "Clothes inside the screened house, on the shelves. Perishables in the fridge, and cans and bottles in the chest outside. There's a box with a lid nailed to the palm, and the soap and shampoo go there."

"We're really going to stay here?"

Ira let out his breath quietly. She didn't sound mad; she sounded fascinated. "Sure," he answered. "Why not? This is a rather comfortable way to camp out. Lots of luxuries, like running water and refrigeration. No electricity, however. Is that going to be a problem to you?"

"Let me think about it."

He hesitated, then dropped the rope and sat on the edge of the split, leather seat. "Think, then. There's a modern house we can rent, or we can go back to the boat."

She nodded and wandered away, opening the front door of the screen house and going inside, traversing the small space corner by corner, not touching, just looking, staring at the shelves, the bed, which seemed very high, the oil lamp.

Like a cat, Ira thought suddenly. A cat in a strange place, checking it out, sniffing, breathing it in.

Diane went on, out the back way. She opened the door of the old refrigerator and looked in, looked into the oven of the stove, into the chest, which held a few pans and utensils. Then on, turning on the shower and jumping back as it sprayed out, opening the door to the outhouse and gazing in amazement at the modern toilet there and the lavatory, complete with a medicine chest. She shut the door and wandered back, going in through the back door of the little house, stopping to hoist herself up to sit on the edge of the bed for a moment. Then she came out to Ira.

"I'll stay. I like it." She smiled. "If I join the Peace Corps, this will seem like luxury. Did you know there's a toilet and lavatory in the outhouse?"

He grinned lazily and got up, beginning again to loosen the load on the buggy. "Certainly. Surely you know I'd never take you to a place without all the modern conveniences?"

THEY SWAM IN THE TWILIGHT, under a sky streaked with rose and gold and pale, sharp green, in a blue sea that whispered along the shore and felt like warm silk. Ira told her there were houses in the woods behind them, but no one appeared, no lights shone through the trees. They might have been the only two people in the world.

Coming up from the sea, they showered under the palm, hung their suits on a bay tree and went inside the screen house to dry each other with rough towels and the heat of passion.

"I can't stand it," Ira said, clutching her close. "Stop teasing me. How much of this do you think I can take?"

"I didn't do anything," she protested. "I just stood here quietly while you dried me."

"Exactly. You stood there, quietly driving me crazy."

She threaded her fingers through the damp hair on his chest. "We can eat later, darling."

"No, dammit! When I start making love to you, I'm not going to stop to cook. Where are my clean shorts?"

Diane sighed. "Don't you know? Oh, never mind. Light the lamp and I'll find them for you."

She sounded so much like an indulgent wife that he didn't know whether to laugh or run like hell. "I'll start dinner," he said briskly. "We're having conch chowder and corn bread. You can set the table."

It pleased her to play at a ridiculous formality. She spread the weather-beaten table with a white cloth, found two discarded pop bottles and set candles in them. She found yellow beach daisies at the edge of the trees and an old conch shell to put them in. And, of course, the silverware from the yacht, the plastic wineglasses, the chilled wine. She arranged everything gracefully, standing back to look, moving the candles to shine on the daisies.

Ira watched her in silence. When he brought the bowls of chowder to the table, the pan of corn bread, the plate of butter, he was careful not to disarrange her setting. Then he stepped back, grabbed a chair and spoke in a bad imitation of an English drawl.

"May I seat you, m'lady?"

Her eyes shot to his. "It's too fussy, Ira? I'm sorry. It does take up a lot of room. I'll clear it off...."

"Don't," he said, surprised. "I like it. I wasn't criticizing. It reminds me of the English nobs in the jungle—having dinner in their evening clothes."

"Oh!" She laughed softly and came forward, a hand on one hip. "In that case, m'lud . . ." With enormous dignity she sat on the weather-beaten chair. He took a chair, his eyes drawn to her elegant face, all soft shadows and golden glow in the candlelight, her blue eyes dark and mysterious, her high cheekbones and subtly contoured lips gleaming. Neither the crooked bump on her nose nor the scar showed, but he already knew it made no difference whether they did or didn't. The effect was always the same when he dared to really look at her, when he allowed it to happen. She leaned forward, cut the corn bread into generous squares, and offered it to him, before taking one for herself. He kept on staring at her, stunned by the way he felt, telling himself it wasn't real; it would go away.

"Ira?"

"Yes? Oh, sure. Thank you. Sorry to keep you waiting. I was thinking, I guess. . . ." He took the square and began to eat. "Be careful with the chowder, it's hot."

He spoke very little during the meal. His silence was puzzling to Diane, but didn't bother her. She was fascinated by the scene, by how they were actually cooking and eating in a jungle. The oil lamps flared and swung in a puff of night breeze, huge moths blundered into the circle of light, small animals rustled and squeaked in the darkness around them. She thought about Yuri and his advice. *Go forth into the world and look for happiness and adventure. Find a man you can share with.* She looked around and her lips curved into a slow smile. If Yuri could see her, he'd approve. He would have liked Ira Nicholson. She glanced across the table and saw that Ira was still watching her.

"That's a secretive smile," he said. "What are you thinking of?"

"Adventures." Yuri's advice was between Yuri and herself. Maybe, someday, if she saw Ira again, if she ever knew him well enough, she would tell him about it.

"Past, present or future?"

Diane laughed. "All of those and all at once. You seem to make things happen. What are those creatures rustling in the grass?"

He smiled. "Grasshoppers."

"Oh." She nodded and smiled. "I should have known."

His smile left when he saw she believed him. He had begun to realize how incredibly little she knew about the natural world. It was as if she'd never been anywhere except the heavily guarded compound where Harrington Roberts lived or Yuri Stephan's tight fortress. Of course, she'd gone to college for that miserable time and she'd gone to work in a concrete and glass tower and ended up owning it. But she'd always lived in one cage or another. Never free until now. He pushed back his chair and got up.

"It's probably a number of different little animals and bugs," he said gently. "Anything from mice to beetles. Things too small and frightened to hunt for food in the daylight. Let's get these dishes done."

Later, with the flaring oil lamps snuffed out and the light of a rising moon shining through the trees, they stripped and got into the high bed. It was firm but comfortable, the top of the mattress level with the windowsill.

"Primitive air conditioning. So you get the full benefit of the breeze," Ira said when she asked. He pulled her over him, so that her hair hung down like a fragrant tent, enclosing their faces, billowing slightly with the breeze. He could see nothing except the glint of her smile, think of nothing except the way she felt—her breasts brushing his chest, the warmth of her slender body, the way she moved, instinctively adjusting herself to his angles and planes, fitting against him. Then he thought of what she had said about the last week being the best, and his arms tightened spasmodically.

"Kiss me, woman."

She bent toward him, slanting her head a little, feeling her way in the darkness.

He felt the warmth of her breath on his mouth, then the lightest touch of lips and the moist heat of her tongue, gently licking his lips apart, coaxing them open. Her tongue entered his mouth, touching his tongue with a curling tip, and he greeted it with a sudden heat, a quick capture, sucking it in, wanting the singular flavor that identified this woman. When her tongue withdrew, he held the kiss with his following tongue, the deep tenderness he felt for her rising with his passion, felt the crazy pounding of their hearts beating together. God, it was good. He relaxed into it, letting it wash over him in a flood of sensual pleasure.

Finally Diane pulled away, gasping for breath, flinging herself onto her back beside him, laughing a little. "Time out for breathing. . . ."

He rolled, rising over her, staring into her face, lit now by the moon. Seeing her clearly made him remember, jolted him with his hidden fear. He tried to make a joke of it. "How can you ask me for a time-out, when you've given me only a week more?"

Her ear caught the real meaning and her soft laughter stilled. "Ira...don't. It's hard enough to leave you. Don't make it worse."

His heart leaped. "You, too? Then...why, Sparrow? Why now?"

She shook her head. "Don't...don't, darling. We have so little time. Let's not fill it with arguments."

"But..."

"Shh. Make love to me." She pulled him down, her hands running over him in desperate, trembling insistence, touching him intimately, imploringly, her lips parting to his kiss.

Her scent was in his nostrils, her hands were caressing him, and his whole, taut body sprang into quivering readiness. He moved to take her and felt her hips rise; her silky legs slipped around him, urging him farther. He took her with a rush, finding her wet and ready, her inner flesh shuddering with desire, closing tight around him. He let out his breath in a gust of satisfaction.

"So good," he whispered, "Perfect. My darling...my passionate love...."

The moon was far to the west and Diane was asleep when Ira thought again of what he had wanted to say to her this evening. He had planned to tell her exactly how he felt. For instance, he had intended to say they suited each other far too well to separate now. It was always a mistake to break up a great combination. He had wanted to point out that she was new at this game and could use a little advice.

He looked at her sleeping face and pulled her closer, settling her head on his shoulder, her hips against his lean belly. Yawning, relaxing at last, he shut his eyes. He could tell her that until she tried looking for another companion, she wouldn't realize how hard it was to find a good match. He could say—with truth—that until now there had never been anyone for him that he wanted to keep. Maybe that would convince her.

12

"THERE IS a very small dragon," Diane whispered, "doing push-ups on the window frame."

Ira opened his eyes, blinked, and concentrated on the window. A horizontal ray of brilliant sunlight shone on the frame, turning the old wood to splintered gold. On it, a tiny, bobbing shadow led his eye to its source. A mottled brown, anole lizard, five inches of cold-eyed, long-jawed ferocity, was displaying. Bobbing his head, pushing up and down on his short legs, the anole raised his chin and thrust out his colorful throat fan, furling and unfurling a glorious flag of flame-orange membrane edged with yellow, glowing and translucent in the bright light.

"That's an anole. A lizard. He's displaying."

Her eyes, startling blue in a morning-pale face, switched to him. "You mean he's showing off?"

"In a way. He's informing the other male lizards that this is his domain and he's all pumped up to defend it. He is also showing his female how good-looking and how strong he is, so she won't go visiting."

Diane laughed. "How efficient. Chasing off the guys and keeping his ladylove. Will he bite?"

"Not us. They're useful around a place. Great insect exterminators. Who's going to make the coffee?"

"I am. I'm going to make our breakfast. How do you light a gas stove?"

"You ask me to light it and then you watch. Want to go swimming first?"

"Oh, yes! I'd love it."

While swimming, they heard the sound of a plane circling, a small, private jet, one of the best, slanting down in a rather steep drop.

"There's a landing strip down there," Ira commented, staring after the plane. "The drug cartel built it, but it's not kept up and it's rough as hell. Someone must be in a hurry to get here. It doesn't seem right, does it? This place is too laid-back for people in a hurry."

"True," Diane said slowly. She was still staring after the plane, wondering at the sense of strain she suddenly felt. In a moment she shook the feeling off, knowing that the plane only reminded her of the world she had left, the world of big business, of chartered jets and cutthroat deals. She didn't have to go back to that. "I'm hungry," she said, turning toward shore. "I'll go start breakfast."

They had finished the meal and were walking down to the beach buggy, when a Jeep came out of the woods a quarter mile on and came toward them, fast.

"That's Frank Bowers," Ira said, stopping to watch. "He runs the new club here. I wonder who he's looking for."

"Me," Diane said painfully. "He's looking for me. That's Paul with him."

"Damn!" Ira stared at the small, thin man beside the driver. "I'll have Jack Griffith's skin for this!" Without thinking, he took Diane's arm and thrust her behind him, standing ready, his thick shoulders hunched forward, his big hands clenched, his face hard. The Jeep came to a stop, the driver looking at Ira in sudden doubt, Paul turning red as he climbed down. Ira bristled, ready to pounce.

"What in the hell are you doing here, Stephan?"

Watching, Diane was irresistibly reminded of the anole. Ira was definitely displaying. *My territory. My woman.*

"I'm sorry, but I have to talk to Diane. I couldn't wait any longer." The red was fading from Paul's face, leaving it pale and sweating. He was dressed in his usual gray suit, white shirt and narrow, dark tie, his small feet in highly polished, black elevator shoes. He looked completely out of place, as if he hadn't planned to come here; as if, at this particular moment, under the feral glare of Ira Nicholson's furious eyes, he wished himself almost anywhere else.

"The last time you talked to Diane," Ira said tightly, "I wanted to break your neck. Insult her again and I will."

"Insult her? That's the last thing I want to do. I've come to apologize...." Paul leaned to the side, trying to see around Ira and catch Diane's eye without coming any closer to those fists. "Please, Di, you've got to listen. Anna and I need you—and so does the corporation. It's going under...."

Diane sighed, took a step forward, slipped her hand into Ira's tense fingers and gave them a squeeze. "I'll listen," she said to Paul, "because of Anna, not because of the corporation. It's sold. Come up with us to the shade." She glanced at the driver, still in the Jeep. "We'll bring Paul back, Mr. Bowers. You don't need to wait."

Bowers looked from Paul to Ira. It was plain that he thought there would be trouble. "I don't mind waiting," he said finally. "I'll be right here, Mr. Stephan."

Paul nodded. He looked relieved, though when Diane turned to walk back up with Ira he came right along, nervous but more than willing. Diane expected a tirade from him when he saw the camp, but he only eyed the place with absolute incredulity. Ira was silent, furious, refusing to look at Diane, but also refusing to leave her side. When she took Paul to the table, Ira sat between them, his eyes narrowed and icy cold.

"Now, Paul." Diane's voice was cool and brisk. "What's the problem?"

"The sale of the Stephan Corporation fell through," Paul said, so rapidly that the words ran together. For a moment Diane was confused. Then the sense of it came to her and she gasped.

"How?"

Blotches of red appeared again on Paul's face and neck. "I sued to stop it, on the grounds that Father was not in his right mind when he gave it to you.... Just remember, I was very angry about you selling it, and for that matter I still think you could have asked my opinion—" He stopped abruptly as Ira's shaggy head swung toward him. "No, wait. Forget the excuses. I was stupid. I may as well admit it. Anyway, my lawyer got an injunction."

Diane's eyes widened. "And you won? I don't believe it."

Paul moved restlessly. "The suit hasn't come up yet. But the buyers pulled out. They had the right. The closing had been set and the injunction stopped it. They were furious and didn't want their money tied up in a family quarrel that might go on for years."

Diane sighed. "A lousy trick, Paul. You let your temper ruin the sale. But you can't win your suit, and I can try again. Henry Wilton can run it as well as anyone until then."

Paul coughed and looked down at his hands, twisting on the tabletop. "It won't be there, Diane. I told you— it's going under. They're already letting employees go, and the big investors are pulling their money out. Wil-

ton says the company can't operate without those funds."
He looked up, his eyes scornful. "Those men are running scared. Where's their loyalty? They made their fortunes with Yuri Stephan."

"You have a nerve to speak of loyalty, Paul," Ira said, feeling tired and utterly disgusted. He turned to Diane, who looked sick. "I've seen this happen before. Someone whispers that the buyers found something rotten in the deal. That gets around, and people start saying if men like that won't risk their money, the little guys had better get out. It spreads like wildfire, Sparrow. You may not salvage any of it."

Diane met his eyes. "I know. But I have to try." She stared at Paul. "You and I, Paul, can get by nicely on what we have, but there are two hundred employees and their families who depend on their jobs. You might have thought of them."

"I realize that," Paul said stiffly. "I said I was sorry, and I meant it. Do you want to fly back with me?"

Diane turned to Ira. "That's an idea. There's no reason why you should have to go."

Ira thought about the plane and the rough strip. Two planes had already crashed on takeoff from Norman's Cay. Of course, Paul would have hired a good pilot, but... "There's no reason for me to stay here, either. And I'd rather take you myself. I'll have you there by tomorrow noon." He turned to Paul. "Just to satisfy my curiosity—how in hell did you find us?"

Paul squirmed. "Edie Laurant called and told me Diane was on Eleuthera. I flew there first. I had to tell Griffith it was a case of life or death before he gave me your location." He looked at Diane again. "I would have said anything I had to say, Di. Anna and I both want it made right, and you're the only one who can do it."

Diane looked at him sharply. "There's one thing you can do. You can withdraw that suit. And make it public! If it looks like the family is making peace, it may help."

Paul stood up, brushing sand from his suit. "I'll be glad to do that, Di." He took Diane's hand into his and squeezed it emotionally. "Anna will be so happy. She's hardly spoken to me in the last month. And, I almost forgot—the first chance you get, I really need you to look over my stock portfolio and bring it up to date. . . ."

Ira turned on his heel, muttering to himself and went into the screened house to start packing.

At noon he carried the last of the boxes onto the yacht and sat down to eat the salad and sandwiches Diane had made. She brought coffee and cups and sat down with him, silent because he was silent, feeling wary and wondering. He was angry, she knew. In the past she would have felt she was somehow to blame for that, but paradoxically, he had given her enough self-confidence, so that she felt no guilt for his temper. She thought of how many things—good things—he'd taught her. She would never forget him.

"If we leave in the next hour," Ira said, finishing his coffee, "we'll be across the Tongue of the Ocean before dusk. We can anchor up for the night off Andros, and head for Cat Cay in the morning. We'll refuel there, turn in our permit and flag, and be in Miami an hour later."

"Thank you. This is a bother for you, I know."

He gave her a hard look. Her voice was cool and calm; her face held the wary reserve he remembered from the first time they met, making his heart ache. She had withdrawn from him. She was still with him physically, but her mind had already jumped ahead to the problems of the business she had helped build. For the first time he was finding out what it was like to lose a lover he still wanted. Beaten out, he thought wryly, by nothing more than a business crisis. He pushed back his chair and stood up, a bitter taste in his mouth.

"It's all right, Sparrow. It's more or less what we planned, isn't it? A month's cruise, slightly extended."

She made herself smile cheerfully. "It's been wonderful, Ira. You've made a terrific difference in my life."

He kept a tight control on himself. "My privilege, my pleasure, too. You're a lovely woman, Diane."

"Thank you." She rose and began taking plates and cups from the table to the galley, glancing through the windows as he left the saloon and went forward to untie the lines to the dock. How easily he accepted their parting, she thought, and how hard it was for her. But then he'd had a lot of practice.

Looking at it calmly, she decided it was good that this problem with the corporation had come up now. It forced her to leave him, and, even better, would keep her very busy. She would need that. She looked up and saw Ira entering the wheelhouse from the deck and sitting down. The yacht was drifting away from the dock, the engines coughed and caught, and all at once they were leaving. She put down the dish she held and went, almost running, to burst onto the aft deck and look behind them.

The small island lay dreaming in the noonday sun, the white scallops of beach empty, the turquoise and blue water shimmering, reflecting the palms. Diane thought of the camp, of candles in pop bottles, daisies in a shell and British nobs in the jungle. She remembered the rustling that went on in the grass at night and that it wasn't grasshoppers. She smiled, thinking of the tiny, fierce anole. She had loved it all; she had found a kind of life that fascinated her, and all in so little time. "I'll be back," she promised under her breath. "I've got to come back. I've only begun to live."

She went below to sort through the things they had brought back aboard, letting the deep, distant rumble of the *Sea Fever*'s engines soothe her. She put away Ira's clothes and everything else from the boat, but her own clothes and personal items she left in their bags, ready to be taken off tomorrow. When she finished, the sight of the bags piled together and waiting depressed her, so she left, going up to sit with Ira. He greeted her with a reserved and thoughtful look.

"Wasn't Stanton Rogers one of the men in that foursome that backed out of buying the Stephan Corporation?"

She nodded. "Yes. The others were George Hill, Alfred Black and Robinson Murray. We were pleased. They were the kind of men we wanted."

"I can understand that. They're all solid men, though Hill and Black have the reputation of being a little too cautious. But when Rogers wants something, he's usually a bull about getting it. I bet he raised hell when the others insisted on backing out."

Diane looked at him, considering what he had said, and then nodded. "You think I should contact him."

"It can't hurt. He has money and influence, and he may still want a chance at buying in. If word got around that he's still interested, it would be a boost." He caught the surprised gratitude in her blue eyes. "It's just a thought," he added gruffly. "It might help. But one way or another, you'll do it. I'm sure of it."

She smiled, leaning forward and putting a slender hand on his arm. "Thank you. That's a good idea—I hadn't thought of it—just one more in a long list of favors you've done for me."

His pulse had jumped at the mere touch of her hand, his throat had thickened. He wanted to ask a favor of her—*Don't leave me.* He was, he thought wildly, ready to make a commitment if that was what she wanted. Instead he said, "It was my pleasure." Like a parrot, he thought gloomily. Like a broken record. But at least it was true. It had been a pleasure.

THEY ANCHORED THAT NIGHT in a small bay on the north end of Andros, ate steaks Ira had bought to grill at the camp, drank too much wine in an effort to keep their spirits up, and went to bed late and dizzy. The next morning Ira went directly to the wheelhouse with his coffee and, after warming the engines to cruising speed and plotting his course to Cat Cay, shoved the throttles to the wall. The yacht leaped up and planed, leaving a rooster tail of foam all the way to Cat Cay, Bimini and then to Miami. This was a day Ira wanted to have behind him.

It wasn't until the *Sea Fever* was tied in a slip at the Biscay Yacht Basin, and Diane had gone up to the dock master's office to call Alycides and then come back to take the bags Ira was handing up, that he said anything personal. He hadn't meant to. He had decided it would be better simply to say goodbye and wish her luck. But what he said came out by itself as he passed up the last case.

"If you'd like," he suggested in a neutral tone, "we could get together again—once this business is over."

Diane stood there with the case in her hands, staring down at his still, nearly expressionless, bronzed face, the half-bare, muscular body she knew so well, and felt as if a giant hand had squeezed her heart and driven it up into her throat. "That . . . that's a thought," she got out finally. "I'll call you."

Just then Alycides purred up in the long Mercedes-Benz and got out, his silver hair waving in the shore breeze and his dark face serious as he looked along the docks. Diane hailed him and he came toward them, followed by Big John, who had seen the yacht come in and recognized it. The three men took the bags to the car, Big John talking to Ira all the way, and Alycides jumped to help Diane into the car and stow the bags around her. All Ira could do was stand back and lift a hand in farewell as they purred away.

Big John grinned as the Mercedes-Benz disappeared. "Well, how was it? Classy-looking gal there."

Ira looked at him and looked away. "Yes."

"Yes? Is that all you can say? Must have been boring."

"No."

Big John laughed. "Okay, it's none of my business. You going to see her again?"

"Maybe. She said she'd call me."

"Oh, sure. The old 'Don't call me, I'll call you.' That's the way it goes with those rich dames."

Ira's jaw tightened, his hands clenched and then relaxed. Hitting Big John wouldn't solve anything. For that matter, he might be right.

WEAVING EXPERTLY through the heavy traffic, Alycides's eyes sought the rearview mirror.

"You seem very tired, *hija*."

"I'm worried about the business."

"Señora Brodorski has told us. You have had many calls. Luz has written down the names. Have you been well?"

She smiled at his dark, troubled eyes in the mirror. "Yes, very well. Where we went was beautiful and relaxing."

"Good! But I am glad you came home."

"If you are worried about the house, Alycides, I have a plan."

"A plan?"

"Yes. What I am about to do will put me in debt, and if I fail, someone might take the house. We can't risk that. So, do you understand the term life estate?"

Alycides frowned. "No."

"It is a legal paper that gives a person a lifetime ownership in property. When the person dies, the property goes back to the owner. I will sign these legal papers for you, for Luz and Roberto. You will own the house as long as any of you are alive, and no one can take it away. Naturally, none of you can sell it because it must come back to me or my heirs. Now, do you understand?"

"One question."

"Ask."

"Does it mean you cannot stay in the house?"

Diane laughed. "I can, if you invite me."

"I invite you, *hija.* I implore you." Alycides's dark eyes gleamed in the mirror, his features crinkled by his grin. "Otherwise, who will pay our salaries?"

They were both laughing when they stopped at the bronze gates. The laughter felt good, very good to Diane.

13

ENTERING THE HOUSE where she had lived with and learned so much from Yuri, Diane had a sudden surge of energy. She decided to act at once. She called Henry Wilton and invited him to dinner. "I'll want a rundown of all the losses so far, and a clear picture of what you're expecting down the road," she told him. "From what Paul said, I gather that you've let some of our employees go. Is that true?"

"Yes. A full third, I'm sorry to say."

"Hire them back. You can't run a business with two-thirds of the people you need."

"We can't pay them, Diane."

"We'll find the money, Henry. Have someone call them and ask them to come in tomorrow at 11:00 a.m. for a meeting in the cafeteria. I want everyone else there, too, including the board members."

"Why, for heaven's sake? You'll just upset them."

"You think they aren't upset now? I want them to help me, instead of sitting around, waiting for the ax to fall."

Henry made a sound somewhere between a groan and a laugh. "All right. Believe me, if you pull this out of the fire, I'll know I've seen a miracle."

Hanging up, Diane tried to remember where Stanton Rogers lived. It was either Tampa or Saint Petersburg, though he had business interests all over Florida and might be in any large city at the moment. Well, Henry would know. She started for the kitchen to tell Luz they were having company for dinner, when the phone rang.

"Hello?"

Her father's high voice came on. "Is that you, Diane? I heard you've let Yuri's business go to hell since he died. That's not right, you know. He was proud of that corporation."

Diane sighed. She was too beat to argue, and besides, for once he was right. She had been careless, and might as well be honest enough to admit it. "Yes, Father, I do know, and I'm sorry. But it wasn't all my fault, though I doubt you'll believe that."

Surprisingly, Harrington Roberts laughed. "Oh, yes, I do. I know one of the buyers, and he told me what happened. He was badly disappointed. He wanted that buy."

"Which one?" Diane asked, alert. "Stanton Rogers?"

"No. Robinson Murray. You know him. He used to be around when you were growing up. He likes skeet."

"His hair was red then," Diane said slowly, "and he was a pretty good shot. I'd forgotten that."

Her father laughed again. "He hasn't forgotten. He didn't like being beaten by a thirteen-year-old female."

"Did I do that?"

"You did. If you're thinking of asking a favor of him, forget it. He still refers to you as that nasty brat. When are you coming to see me?"

"Tomorrow evening," Diane answered, and, thinking fast, added, "if you'll ask Robinson Murray to dinner."

"You'll never get Rob to pull you out of this, young lady, even if he liked you. He can't afford to go it alone."

"I wouldn't expect that of anyone. Will you ask him?"

"I will. But I warn you, you're going to fall flat on your face."

"I'm already flat on my face," Diane said recklessly. "So I've nothing to lose. I'll see you then."

Diane went through the house and into the kitchen, where Alycides's wife Luz greeted her with a formal bow and a warm smile. *"Como está usted, señorita?"*

Luz, in her sixties, with silver-streaked, black hair, a round, pleasant face and a shape like a five-foot pillow, spoke English, but preferred her own melodic language. Diane humored her when she had time to waste. This wasn't one of those days. She hugged her instead.

"I'm fine. *¡Muy bueno, gracias, muy amable!* Now, speak English. We are having my friend Henry Wilton to dinner this evening. I hope you remember what foods he likes."

"Fish," Luz said, only a little disappointed by the order. "Any food from the sea. And fruit. He crazy for fruit and melon. I know what to fix."

"Good. Now I want the list you made of the people who have called."

"It is on the table of the *teléfono*."

Almost all the calls were from employees of the Stephan Corporation. Workers, she noted, who were in the less important positions and the most likely to be let go. She had always encouraged the employees to come to her with problems about their jobs, so they had been calling her for help and had been put off by Luz, who was anything but tactful on the *teléfono*. The thought made her heart sink. She simply had not acted in a responsible manner. Not at all. She had been too anxious to—to fling herself into life. Or to fling herself into Ira Nicholson's bed? Dammit, she *had* to win this battle—for them, for Yuri, for her own pride.

She scanned the list again, comforted by the knowledge that someone at the Stephan building was already calling the fired employees and telling them to come in tomorrow. There were other names: her father, twice; Anna; and a few names she didn't recognize. One of them, a Sam Rogers, had called three times and left three different numbers. Sam Rogers? Sam? She turned and ran into the kitchen, list in hand.

"This name, Luz. Sam Rogers. Are you sure it was Sam?"

Brows raised, Luz left the melon she was cutting and came to stare at the list, wiping her wet hands on her apron. "Oh, that the one who called four, maybe five times—"

"Three," Diane interrupted, annoyed. "Three times. I asked if you were sure of the name."

"Four, five times," Luz said stubbornly. "But only three numbers he left. His name sound like Sam or Sammon." She giggled abruptly. "Sammon a fish, *sí?*"

"Salmon a fish," Diane said and winced. Now Luz had her doing it. "Could it have been Stan or Stanton?"

"Sure, why not?"

Why not, indeed. Diane let out her breath and smiled. "Thanks, Luz. That was what I needed to know." She went back into the hall, walking on air. Uncertain air. Stanton Rogers must have been interested in a deal, but he might have given up by now. Still, it was worth a try. Ira's advice had always paid off.

Ushered in by Alycides on the dot of seven, Henry Wilton looked tired. Diane handed him a drink and kissed his cheek.

"Henry, I apologize. You were absolutely right—I should have stayed here until the sale was completed. I might have been able to keep Paul from tossing in that monkey wrench."

Henry smiled weakly. "I doubt it. Anna tried, and she has more influence with him than anyone else. But you don't need to apologize to me—I made some very bad moves myself."

"So we both made mistakes. Now we'll work together. Come, let's stop blaming ourselves and eat. Luz has made all your favorite dishes."

Once seated under the glittering candelabra, Henry Wilton gave Diane a genuine smile. "You look wonderful, rested and healthy. Younger than ever. You had a good time?"

"A very good time." She had no intention of talking about Ira Nicholson, so she went on, fast. "I saw a good bit of the Bahamas, did some shooting, some diving, some sightseeing. Fortunately, Paul was able to trace me by getting in touch with some friends. Tell me, has Paul withdrawn his suit?"

"He has. The announcement will be in tomorrow's *Herald*."

"And have you contacted the employees that were let go?"

"Almost all. A few have already taken other jobs, but most of them will be there. They seemed rather excited."

"Good." Diane settled to her first course with a feeling that all at once things were coming together, combining in a way that had the magical touch of the old master, almost as if Yuri himself were directing this ploy. Yuri had always been able to balance men, ideas, facts and prejudices and make them work for him. He'd had an unerring sense of good theater. She smiled at Henry. "Do you realize that Yuri would have been in his element with this crisis?"

"That's so true. He would have charmed those birds right into his hands." He sat looking at her and beaming, then turned serious again. "May his spirit guide you. You're going to need all the help you can get."

Luz came in with the main course and they fell silent until she had served the baked snapper, stuffed with crabmeat, and a spinach and mushroom salad. They both began to eat hungrily, but after a few moments Diane laid down her fork.

"I must ask you not to deny nor argue about any statement I may make tomorrow, Henry. Not even if you feel I'm making impossible, pie-in-the-sky promises."

Henry sighed. "You're an incurable optimist, Di. Please keep it solid. Don't build up their hopes."

"One more suggestion like that and you'll be barred from the proceedings," Diane said, only half teasing. "Eat your dinner and resolve to keep your mouth shut tomorrow."

Henry gave a short laugh. "All right. You have my word. But when you've seen the facts and figures I brought with me tonight, you may alter your plans yourself."

"I may alter my plans, but I won't alter my attitude," Diane returned. "We're going to win."

"I won't fight that. I wish I had the same confidence."

They spent two hours in the library, where Yuri had set up an office, going over the reports of the debacle.

"We haven't lost as many clients as I thought," Diane said as they finished. "But we will if this keeps up. I see those big subdivisions are dropping out as soon as their contracts expire. And the main loss—the invested money in the Land and Home Loan Company—is crippling. We'll have to make that up. Have you talked to the banks?"

"They're willing to take over our mortgage," Henry said dryly. "They are not willing to make us a loan so we can stay in the mortgage business."

Diane nodded. "That makes sense. Why should they help us compete with them? All right. We'll find another way."

"How?"

"I can't tell you how yet. I'm still feeling my way."

Henry stood, gathering papers and shaking his head. "You aren't making me any less nervous, Diane. Who will invest in a failing business? Can you be more explicit?"

"I wish I could, but you'll just have to trust me." Walking him to the door, she knew he didn't and wouldn't, until she came up with a solution that pleased him. Only Yuri, she thought, would have put his trust in her. Yuri and Ira Nicholson? *You'll do it*, Ira had said. *I'm sure of it*.

Going up to her luxurious bedroom, with its wide bed and silken sheets, Diane was lonelier than she had ever been in her life.

A KNOCK ON HER DOOR wakened Diane at seven the next morning and a maid entered, bringing a tray with coffee and *The Miami Herald*. Standard procedure, but this time Diane picked up the paper before the coffee. It was there on the front page of the financial section: "Paul Stephan Withdraws Lawsuit against His Late Father's Partner." And beneath that: "Opens Way for Sale of Stephan Corporation."

Sitting up in her bed, feeling tousled and sleepy-eyed, Diane sipped coffee and read the story. Paul had done it up brown. He was quoted as saying the lawsuit had been a "stupid mistake," caused by a misunderstanding. He went on to say he owed Diane Roberts an apology; he mentioned her "amazing business acumen" and gave her credit for keeping up the high standards of the corporation for the past five years, adding, ". . . while increasing the intrinsic worth of my father's other holdings, which benefitted both my sister's family and me." Diane laughed at that. Paul was making sure she didn't forget his request to update his stock portfolio.

The story was more than she'd hoped for, and made a wonderful beginning for this momentous day. Now to try those three numbers for Stanton Rogers. Of course, she'd have to wait—maybe she should make it noon—so he would have seen or heard the news story. Whatever. *Play it by ear*, she told herself. *By impulse.* So far that was working. She threw back the covers, heading for the shower.

"Yes, sir, Miss Roberts is at home, but she is still in her room. Yes, sir, I'll tell her." Alycides turned from the hall telephone and saw Diane, poised on the stairs. "That was Mr. Paul. He said he would be at the Brodorski house."

"Thanks. I'll call him after I've had breakfast." She paused. "If Mr. Wilton calls, let me know. Tell any others I'll call back when I can."

"I understand, *hija.*" Alycides beamed at her. "There will be many. *The Miami Herald* made you famous this morning."

Diane laughed and went on into the dining room, wondering just what effect the news story would have on the investors who had defected from the corporation. To get them back, the story would have to be followed by encouraging signs. Sitting down to icy melon, she thought of asking a reporter to attend the meeting at 11:00 a.m. It was risky. If the meeting went badly, it could sink her campaign. But if it went well... She smiled and picked up her spoon.

While she ate, the faint ringing of the telephone was almost constant. Alycides came in once to inform her that Henry had called, but had said not to disturb her, he would call again. When she went into the hall later, he handed her the list of callers. She looked and gasped.

"Damn! Oh, no!" She saw Alycides's face fall and shook her head. "Not your fault, Aly. I should have told you that if Mr. Rogers called, I'd talk to him. Did he say where he'd be?"

"I asked for a number, *hija*. He said he would be busy for a few hours and would call again."

"And I," Diane mourned, "will be at that meeting."

"I told him you would be at the Stephan building until afternoon. He said he would talk to you later, then."

"Fine! Just right, Aly. Thank you." She went on, list in hand, to the telephone.

THE CAFETERIA Yuri had built for his employees was midway up the soaring tower of the corporation. It took up most of the floor, along with a lounge, an office and examining room for the company nurse and an exercise room. The dining area was lighted by windows on three sides, providing an excellent view of Biscayne Bay.

When Diane, accompanied by Henry Wilton and Henry's secretary, stepped into the cafeteria, no one in the huge crowd seemed to be gazing at the view. They were all talking, laughing, moving from one group to another, being sociable. Diane stared and it hit her. They thought the crisis had passed. The mere fact that all the fired employees had been asked back had done that.

"Good heavens," Henry muttered. "They think it's a party."

"Good sign," Diane replied and squeezed his arm. "Try a smile yourself, Henry. You might feel better." Her quick eyes found a photographer near the east windows, snapping group shots. She nudged Henry and indicated the camera with a tip of her head. "See that? Either smile or leave, dammit. We don't want any doleful faces in the newspaper."

"You didn't ask the press in?"

"Of course I did. It's news, isn't it?"

"But—what if an argument breaks out? It would be spread all over the paper. . . ."

Diane grasped his hands and turned him toward her, with his back to the room. She smiled sweetly into his contorted face. "Now who," she asked, "is going to argue with me? No one else but you would dare." She held his stubborn gaze, thanking her lucky stars she had called in the press. She could see in his eyes that he actually had intended to argue, once the meeting began and the rest of the board was present.

"Dammit," Henry said finally. "I wouldn't dare, now. But you know you're wrong to encourage—"

"Shhh! They've spotted us." She smiled and held out both hands as the other members of the board came up.

Someone had arranged a speakers' table in the middle of the east wall. There was a place of honor for Diane and seats on either side for the board. When they all sat down, the rest of the crowd scrambled for places at the remaining tables, though some ended up standing along the walls. Diane looked out over the sea of expectant faces and suddenly her stomach sank, her heart began banging against her ribs and her throat closed up. They looked so happy, so confident. What if she was wrong? What if she couldn't turn this disaster around? Why had she thought she could? All she had considered was that her employees needed her, were counting on her. . . .

She stood, looking at the smiles, smiling back.

"I'm counting on you in this crisis," she said warmly. "And you know you can count on me. We're all graduates of the Yuri Stephan method of doing business, and that means we don't just work together—we stick together! Right?"

"R-r-right!" A swelling growl of approval washed over her, and she grinned.

"All *right!* You came here, hoping to hear some good news. Especially you people who got the bad news last month. So here it is—no, wait! How many of you saw the *Herald* today?"

There was another affirmative roar, some whistling and a lot of clapping. Sudden warmth burst in Diane's heart. Tears heated her eyes. She stood straighter, looking at all the beaming, enthusiastic faces.

"I don't know why I thought I had to tell you anything," she said. "You've always known and cared about this business as much as I do. And so you already know that we're on the mend after a very bad time. Mistakes have been made, like in any family, but we're going to get through it fine. Now let me tell you why. It's because we're fixing the biggest mistake of all. We're rehiring everyone who was laid off. We need your skills and knowledge, we need your loyalty and we need every one of you! Remember what Yuri used to say.... Whatever happens, happens to *us.* Are you with me?"

Pandemonium. Pounding on tables, clapping, whistling and cheering went on long after Diane sat down; went on until Henry Wilton, smiling in spite of himself, stood up and waved his arms for quiet. Gradually the noise died away.

"Thank you," Henry said clearly, "on behalf of Miss Roberts and also on behalf of the board of directors. That was a wonderful vote of confidence. We will try to deserve it." He cleared his throat to begin again and caught Diane's wary look. He smiled at her and turned back to the crowd. "In celebration of this good news today, you're invited to have lunch on us."

Leaving, Diane and Henry squeezed into an already crowded elevator along with the *Herald* photographer and a young woman reporter. Wriggling to a place beside Diane, the reporter gazed at her with admiration.

"You ought to go into politics, Miss Roberts. You had those people in the palm of your hand." She chuckled. "You obviously know it's in the voice, not the words. You really project warmth and sincerity. I think they believed you."

"They know me," Diane said gently, "better than you do."

"Oh? You mean you really won't cut down your force if necessary?"

"We'll sink or swim together. I don't lie to my friends."

There was silence until the elevator slowed to a stop at the main floor. As they emerged in the reception hall, a man touched Diane's arm. "Miss Roberts? I'd like a word with you."

She turned. The man who had spoken was big, very fit, with a distinguished, strong face and iron-gray hair. He seemed very familiar, she couldn't place him. "I'm sorry. I'll call you as soon as I can. This is a very busy day for me."

He nodded. "I expect it is. My congratulations, by the way, on how you handled that situation upstairs. It is also a busy day for me, Miss Roberts. You've seen me before in the boardroom here, but I'm afraid you've forgotten it. I'm Stanton Rogers."

Diane gasped, then said the first thing that came into her head. "How did you get into that meeting?"

Rogers grinned. "I'm known to be both innovative and versatile, Miss Roberts. Ask your friend Ira Nicholson."

Diane looked around. The others had gone on, except for Henry, who stood a few yards away, looking as if he wanted to join them. Of course, he knew who Rogers was. She turned her back and spoke to Rogers again.

"You've heard from Ira?"

"This morning, early. He called and gave me some good ideas and encouragement. Now, can we talk?"

Diane's mind was racing. Her plans for the evening, with the dinner at her father's house and the chance to talk to Robinson Murray, were foremost in her mind. She needed to talk to both Rogers and Murray.... She looked up again and smiled.

"I'm having dinner at my father's house this evening, and Robinson Murray is supposed to be there. Would you like to join us?"

"Rob's a friend of mine," he said, smiling ruefully, "but he's been known to try to get ahead of me on a deal. I accept if only to keep my foot in the door."

"Oh, fine! Then . . ." She stopped, laughing a little. "I should have asked—do you mind being frisked?"

"Frisked?"

Diane nodded. "Searched for weapons." She saw that he still didn't understand, which meant he didn't know who her father was. "My father is Harrington Roberts, Mr. Rogers. You probably know he has some peculiar ideas."

Rogers stared at her, then chuckled. "I've never been frisked, but I don't mind. May I pick you up?"

"I'll pick you up, at seven. Where are you staying?"

He named a place on Key Biscayne. Diane nodded and left, joining Henry and continuing outside, where Alycides waited to take her home. Standing by the car, squinting in the glare of the noon sun, Henry looked pale and half-angry.

"You could have called me over," he said. "There might have been a chance to mend some fences. Why did he come?"

Diane glanced at Henry and looked away. No other man in Henry's position would have waited to be asked over. It came to her that while Henry had been a wonderful figurehead as chairman of the board, he had never been capable of the job she'd given him. He had no daring, no intuition, no real courage when it came to hard decisions. She should have realized that. She would have, she thought, if she hadn't been so damned anxious to leave.

"I suppose," she answered him, "he was curious. I think he's still interested in the Stephan Corporation. Since I'm seeing him tonight, I'll find out."

"He asked you for a date?"

Diane laughed. "Don't be so old-fashioned, Henry. I asked him."

14

Dismissing Alycides for the evening, Diane drove the small Mercedes-Benz to the Stanton Rogers condo, arriving at precisely seven o'clock.

"I'll be glad to drive, if you like," Stanton offered.

"Thank you. But it will be easier for me. My father's house is rather out-of-the-way."

He nodded and got in. She noted his light gray slacks, the white, Irish linen sport shirt, the muted, gray-blue jacket. A lesser man, invited to the home of Harrington Roberts, would have put on a formal suit in spite of the heat. Stanton Rogers was a confident man. She liked that, but realized it would make her job harder. He wouldn't be easy to lead.

She drove west across the busy, traffic-choked bridge and into the last of the hot light of the June day. While the traffic demanded her careful attention, she was conscious of Roger, the faint, tangy odor of his shaving lotion, and his inspecting gaze going over her.

"Ira tells me," he said suddenly, "that you're a crack shot. Frankly, it doesn't seem possible."

Diane glanced at him in surprise. She hadn't expected a personal remark. "What else did he tell you, Mr. Rogers?"

"Not nearly enough, Miss Roberts, in spite of my many questions. May I call you Diane?"

"Of course. Which do you prefer, Stanton or Stan?"

"Stan." He smiled again and settled back comfortably. "Tell me about your father. I've heard all the usual drivel about him, but I discount that sort of thing."

"Don't. What you've heard is probably true."

After a moment of astonished silence, Stan laughed. "Perhaps it is. His daughter appears to be a bit different, too. Then you meant it when you said I'd be frisked?"

Diane smiled. She was gradually moving into the Miami streets, heading toward Old Cutler Road. "Actually, you won't be personally searched unless you set off an alarm when we enter the house. And even then you have a choice."

"Which is?" He was clearly amused, enjoying this.

"Be searched," she answered, "or leave with an armed escort."

"How is it that Robinson Murray knows him well enough to get in?"

"He's a longtime friend. But he doesn't get in without the same safeguards." She glanced over and then away. "I go through the electronic detector, Stan."

"*You?*"

She laughed, relaxing. "My father likes to make a point, Stan. When he says he's suspicious of everyone, he means it. Now let's talk about something else."

"Great idea." Rogers sat up, laying an arm along the back of the seat. "I've got an offer for you. I know as much as you do about what's happened to the Stephan Corporation, and I know it's bad. But I pride myself on putting things back together after a jolt like that. Are you ready to sell?"

Diane laughed again. "Not," she said, "at what you're ready to offer me. Once I heal the wound you four brave men gave me when you pulled out, then I sell."

Rogers had the grace to look embarrassed, she saw. He settled back again and stared at the passing traffic. "Pulling out wasn't my idea," he said, "nor Murray's. But Hill and Black insisted." His head turned toward her once more. "You realize the time and money it'll take to put the business back on track?"

"No, I don't. And neither do you. Yuri taught me to view every problem as unique, with its own unique solution. I'm still studying this one."

He was silent for some time. "I'd forgotten," he said at last, "that I was talking to someone trained by Yuri Stephan. I'll be lucky to come out of this with my shirt on."

Diane chuckled. "Don't be bitter."

He gave her a long, appraising glance, one she found familiar. "If you don't mind personal questions, I'd like to know just what it was that attracted you to Yuri Stephan."

Slowing, Diane turned into a narrow winding lane, then stopped at a tall, solid gate and blew the horn. "Sorry," she said. "I can't think of any reason why you need to know."

"Maybe I'd like to try attracting you myself. You're a fascinating woman, Diane." He grinned at her incredulous glance. "You'd have to be," he went on, "to interest a man like Stephan for so long, and to keep Ira Nicholson hanging around, waiting for you to call."

Was he? Was Ira still there because he wanted to hear from her? Diane felt a shockingly strong wave of longing sweep over her, painful in its intensity. For a moment she could see Ira in her mind, as clearly as if he stood before her in the twilight. That wonderful, lean, masculine body. His quick grin, the hot, golden look in his eyes when he took her into his arms. It was like a hammer blow to her heart. How she missed him! She forced herself to look at Stanton Rogers, and a dull anger built inside her, because he had somehow breached her defenses.

"That's over," she said harshly, more to herself than to him. "In the past. Right now I'm interested in my business and my employees, not in flirtation."

He started to answer, but the gates were swinging open, revealing a small guardhouse. Uniformed men, wearing sidearms, came forward. They nodded at Diane and peered inside, rather casually at first. Then one of them drew his gun and opened the passenger door.

"Miss Roberts," he said in a soft, hurt tone, "you didn't mention that you were bringing a guest. Please, sir, would you mind coming with me?"

Fifteen minutes later Rogers emerged from the guardhouse, both his clothes and his temper plainly ruffled. He climbed into the car and spoke gruffly.

"Did you plan this?"

"No. But I do apologize. With everything that's been going on, I simply forgot to call. The guards operate on the premise that any unannounced person coming inside may have forced the driver to bring him."

"I see." He braced his legs, raising himself from the seat and trying to tuck in his shirt evenly, his frown vanishing. He laughed. "So, I've had a new experience. I've not only been frisked—I've been subjected to a body search. The men were polite, but they were thorough. If I needed guards, I'd hire them."

"There," she said as they rounded a wooded curve, "is the house. The men at the gate have called ahead by now, so you'll be expected. We'll sail right through. Looks like a prison, doesn't it?" She waved a hand at the three-storied pile of carved and tessellated stone that loomed into the night.

"Perhaps," Stan said slowly, "but rather magnificent."

Parking, they walked together to the front entrance and entered a wide and lavish foyer through a doorway with no sign of any electronic device, but two more uniformed men watched closely and only turned away after they were inside. An attractive, middle-aged woman in a black silk skirt and white blouse came up to them, smiling.

"Your father is waiting for you in the library, Miss Diane. Mr. Robinson Murray is with him."

"Thank you, Cora. This is Stanton Rogers."

Cora extended a hand. "Good evening, Mr. Rogers."

Diane led the way to the library. The two men who waited inside the large and richly furnished room were as unlike as any two men could be: Robinson Murray, a huge, untidy and overweight man in his fifties, with a singularly friendly smile on his red face; and Harrington Roberts, who looked like a sixty-year-old, discontented boy. Small and thin, wearing a brilliantly white, summer-weight suit, the crease of the trousers sharp enough to cut, he had a stringy crop of damp, yellowish hair and a small-featured, petulant face. He waved a languid hand at Diane as they came in and ignored Stanton Rogers.

"Come here," he said to her, "and kiss your old father. You've taken your time about coming to see me."

Diane went to him and dropped a kiss onto his cheek. "I've been rather busy," she pointed out. "Thanks to Paul Stephan."

"Don't blame it on him. You should have known better." He spoke with relish, rubbing his hands together. "I knew you'd do something stupid, once you owned that business. I tried to warn Yuri years ago not to depend on you."

A familiar pressure began behind Diane's eyes. She turned away, grateful as Robinson Murray introduced Stan to her father. A maid came in with a tray of drinks and she took one, gulping it down. Then all at once a memory surfaced in her mind. She was back on the *Sea Fever*, the day of the sharks, crying over her own, stupid cowardice, admitting to Ira that her father had said all along that she was no damn good. And Ira was holding her. *Believe me*, he had said, *your father is wrong.*

"Aha," Robinson Murray said, touching her arm, "what a lovely young woman you turned out to be, you nasty brat."

Diane turned to him with a small smile. "Still smarting over a skeet score, Mr. Murray. You've a long memory."

Murray's huge, loose body shook with laughter. "That was a major disaster, you know. Your father over there had bet me a thousand that you could beat me, and you damn well did. Now you've turned up with a business I want, and I suppose you'll beat me again—and saddle me with your problems."

"No, I'll not," Diane said in sudden decision. It had come to her that the only way to handle this was to put the sale off—temporarily. Both of these men would try hard to take advantage of the present trouble in the corporation. She wouldn't put up with that kind of manipulation. She still intended to get the original bid, or better it. It was a fair price, in some ways a bargain. She looked up, finding both Murray and Rogers looking at her curiously, waiting to hear more.

"If I have to, I'll build the corporation up again," she told them, "and put out a call for bids, the same way we did it before. Your bid was by no means the highest, you know. The board picked you because they liked your reputation. This time I'll go for the gold and stay with it until the sale is final."

Across the room Harrington Roberts's pale eyes glittered, his knife-thin mouth curved in a sour smile. "That's my girl," he said unexpectedly. "Make 'em sweat." He held up a white birdlike wrist and looked at his watch. "In the meantime, our dinner is being served."

THE MAIN DINING ROOM of Harrington's immense home faced an atrium that lay at the center of the building and contained a pool and gardens. It was a peaceful scene and Diane concentrated on it, sipping her wine and ignoring the rich food piled on her plate. Now that her decision was made and stated, she was able to relax a little. Even the time she might have to give up to bring the corporation back to its former value, she decided, would be therapeutic. If she ever expected to forget Ira Nicholson, she would need the distraction of hard work.

"Don't you think so, Diane?"

She looked up at Robinson Murray, realizing the conversation had gone on without her. "I'm sorry," she said. "I was woolgathering. What was the question?"

He smiled, a trifle condescendingly, she thought. "I said I thought the number of enclosed shopping malls in south Florida had reached its peak, and wondered if you agreed with me. But you've been away for over a month, so I suppose you aren't up on things."

"I'm up on that, Mr. Murray. With Florida's rapidly expanding population and the warm climate, the enclosed and air-conditioned malls will proliferate for years. It's by far the most comfortable way to shop, and people travel miles to spend a day inside. We are currently managing seven large malls scattered along the

West Coast, and I can tell you it's a great investment, given the right location."

Across the table Stanton Rogers picked up the questioning. "Aren't you afraid some of those malls may slip away from you in this troubled time?"

"By the time their contracts come up for renewal," Diane said shortly, "the troubles will be over. Besides, the Stephan Corporation is known to give the best service, and we've a lot of loyal clients. I'm not worried about losing them."

"But the investment money problem—"

"Has been rough," Diane cut in quickly, her eyes going back to Murray. "I freely admit that. One or two men panicked and withdrew their funds. Others thought they knew something and followed. However, I'm no longer worried. We're all contributing, and once the public realizes we're fully funded again, they'll invest."

Murray's heavy eyebrows arched. "*All* contributing? Who is all?"

Diane smiled. "I hoped you'd ask that. Just before I left home this evening, Henry Wilton called me. He was, to put it mildly, excited. Our employees, who have an extremely healthy credit union, held a supplemental meeting after our session this morning, and voted to invest half of their savings in the loan company. It's a tremendous boost." She could see by the expression on Murray's face that he agreed with her last remark and didn't like hearing it. He turned and looked at Stanton Rogers, who grinned ruefully and nodded.

"You can't beat it," Stan said. "It's one hell of an advantage to have your employees show that kind of faith."

"Yes," Murray muttered, obviously shaken. "For one thing, they work harder when they stand to gain from it." He stared at Diane. "I suppose you invested a good sum yourself."

"Of course." She was suddenly enjoying this. Yuri, she thought, would have reveled in it. It was his kind of deal, his kind of pressure. Nothing crooked, just the best arguments, the best moves, coming together, meshing neatly. She looked down the table at her father, who had been silent, listening throughout the conversation. There was an odd expression on his querulous face. Almost, she thought, as if he agreed with her tactics, almost approving.

"Well," Stanton Rogers said into the silence, "I have certain commitments to my own businesses, and therefore I can't afford to pay the full price for yours, Diane. Over to you, Rob." He leaned back, his strong face falling into lines of disappointment.

"Hell," Murray muttered. "I'd be hard put to come up with half of the original price I mean to offer."

"I wouldn't invest five cents in something Diane owned, but I'll put my money on you, Murray," Harrington said peevishly. "Take Rogers as a partner, and I'll take shares in the corporation for the rest of the purchase price. That is, I will, if you all agree to keep it under wraps." He stared around at the three shocked faces and came up with his small, sour smile. "I have no objection to making money, you understand. Just don't expect me to do anything, nor put myself in the public eye. And don't use my name! I like my privacy."

STAN INSISTED ON DRIVING when they left. It was midnight, and he obviously felt protective. "Once you drop me off," he said, "you're fair game for our criminal element. I'll take you to your house and catch a taxi to mine."

Diane was too exhilarated to argue. She got into the passenger seat obediently, gave him directions and sat back to enjoy the ride. Stanton Rogers was an expert driver, handling the car with easy skill and confidence. She thought he probably carried over those qualities into every part of his life.

Not that it mattered to her. She was too busy with her own feelings, with freedom a shimmering, possible dream, lying only a short distance away. A week, perhaps, and the sale would be a reality.

It seemed only a step between her father's house and the Miami traffic, the Miami River and its clots of boats. She tried, hard but unsuccessfully, not to think of Ira. Not to think of their adventure. *When it's over,* she told herself, *it's over.* And it was over, even before they went to that island, that crazy, wonderful, dragon haunted island....

"Now, which causeway?"

She glanced over, embarrassed to be caught dreaming. Stan's grin acknowledged her inattention, and she smiled. "The Venetian is closest."

"Then maybe I'll take the Julia Tuttle."

She realized he meant that flirtatiously, but didn't care. He probably flirted with every woman he met. "It doesn't matter," she said and settled back again, watching the speeding, blinking, vibrating lights of traffic, the throbbing reflections of the Bay, the floodlights on the marble and glass towers that had changed old Miami's downtown to a shining metropolis. Then she began thinking of her next moves. No problem with the contract—they'd agreed to use the one they had signed before, with the other men's names left off. And with her in charge until the sale was completed, there would be no problem about a CEO....

"Is this the street I want?"

Diane sat up, staring at the familiar sign, the quiet, opulent neighborhood among huge trees. "Yes. Turn left, and I'll tell you when to turn again. I truly am sorry, Stan. I'm thinking of everything, except what we're doing."

He nodded, driving on. "I don't mind at all. Naturally you're thinking of the future. I'm doing that myself."

"Of course you are." She yawned, suddenly conscious of a pleasant exhaustion, a feeling that now she could rest, could drop into dreamless sleep. "There," she said, "there is our gate. Just stop and blow your horn."

The gate swung open instantly. "Beautiful," Stan said, driving in. "Impressive. You own it, I understand."

She smiled, her hand on the door. "Come in. I'll make you a nightcap while you call a taxi." She hoped he'd refuse, but saw right away that he wouldn't. He wanted a drink; perhaps he wanted to talk some more.

Alycides opened the door as they walked up the steps, his shaggy, silver and black brows knitted in visible displeasure. Diane gave him an apologetic smile.

"I'm sorry to keep you up so late, Alycides. It was a long, but satisfactory evening."

"It is my duty, *hija,*" Alycides said grimly, "to see you safe inside." His black eyes swept Stanton Rogers critically from head to toe. "I will be in the kitchen if there is something you need."

"I will need nothing I can't get myself. Go to bed."

He grumbled but went, stalking up the stairs in injured silence. Stan looked at Diane and smiled.

"*Hija?* Do you go around collecting fathers?"

Diane laughed. "They volunteer, I think. There's the phone, Stan. If you're as tired as I am, you'll be anxious to get home. While you're waiting, we'll have a brandy—if that suits you."

"Brandy suits me." He watched her leave then reluctantly went to the telephone table. He was in no mood to leave, but she had made her feelings plain.

"I've opened the gate," Diane said, reappearing with two balloon glasses and a squat bottle of brandy. "Which means a bell will sound here in the foyer when the taxi enters. Which also means this is where we'll sit." She sat down on an ornate, tapestry-covered chair and motioned him to one nearby, smiling at his expression. "The safeguards here require a lot of attention. I'm glad to be getting away from them."

"Are you?" Looking immense on the small chair, Stan sipped the brandy and watched her. "Going to sea again? You told me you were through with Ira Nicholson."

"That's true. I did say that." She looked down, swirling her brandy, wondering if, after all, she was strong enough to make it stick. "There are other things to do. I'm free to choose now."

Stan set his empty glass on a small table, centering it carefully. "I've been hoping you'd stay around and give me a chance to be your friend—no, let me be honest—a chance to be more than a friend. Naturally I can't compete with a party stud like Nicholson, but . . ."

"Dammit!" Diane said violently. "Don't call him that! Ira is the finest of friends, the most considerate of lovers, the best of all the men I ever met! Don't you dare put him down!"

They stared at each other in the echoing silence of the large foyer, equally surprised by her outburst. Then, her hand shaking, Diane put down her glass.

"Sorry," she said shakily, looking away. "It's just that . . . Ira is such a—a really great guy. . . ."

"And you're in love with him."

She whirled. "I'm not! We had this agreement . . . I mean, it was understood that we were absolutely not serious!"

Stan nodded. "He was careful to say your, uh, relationship was that of a friend. But I didn't believe him, either."

"Neither of us lie—" She stopped, listening to the melodious tinkle of a bell overhead. "That's your taxi," she added and stood up, relieved to have the conversation over. She smiled and offered her hand as he rose. "I'll see you at the closing, then. It's wonderful to know that men like you and Robinson Murray are taking over Yuri's work."

He had kept her hand as he went to the door and opened it. Standing in the doorway, he grinned down at her. "Even if both of us had to find a silent partner?"

"That won't matter. You'll all make money. . . ." She stopped and raised her brows, realizing what he'd said. "Oh. You have a silent partner, too?"

"Nicholson is putting up half of my share," Stan said casually. "He called and offered a loan for the whole amount, but I talked him into taking shares instead." She saw him look around as the taxi slid to a stop at the steps. "Well, I thought you ought to know. Obviously he did it to help you, and you might like to thank him." He released her hand and touched her cheek with a finger, grinning wryly. "I think you'll find out I was right. In the meantime, good night, and thanks for an illuminating evening."

She stood there in the glow of the hidden, golden lights in the deep shrubbery, until the sound of the taxi faded in the distance and the faint clang of the closing gates came to her ears. She felt frozen, cold with indecision in the warm, June night.

15

THE FORMAL CLOSING of the sale took place one week later. Afterward, leaving the Stephan building in the company of the new owners, Diane turned and looked up, studying the towering marble and glass facade. Deep in conversation, Henry Wilton and Robinson Murray walked on, but Stanton Rogers stopped, raising his brows.

"Regrets?"

"None. But a lot of memories. I grew up in there." She turned back to him and continued toward the outside parking lot. Only owners and board members parked inside. "I'm glad to be handing it over in good shape, Stan."

"Yes. You turned it around at flank speed, mostly due to your influence with the employees. I wish you'd stay. You could name your own salary."

She looked up at him and smiled. "You know better."

He was silent, taking her arm as they entered the parking lot. It was hot, July hot, the tar-based paving beneath their feet molten and giving off waves of heat.

"Take a trip," Stan said. "Somewhere quiet and cool. The mountains are ideal in July. Then in the fall, give it some thought. You'll be bored with nothing important to do."

She laughed. "That's exactly what Henry said when I left before. I suppose it's a natural assumption, but it didn't happen. I was never bored."

They had reached her car, parked in a tree-shaded area, and he opened the door for her. "I can believe that," he said dryly, "considering who you were with. However, there isn't an Ira Nicholson waiting on every street corner. Or in a marina, for that matter. I went down and told him about our agreement, and he said to give you his congratulations. A day or two later his boat was gone. Men like Ira have restless feet."

That jolted her. She got into the driver's seat, turning the air conditioning on high, leaving the door open. "True," she said at last, glad her voice sounded calm. "But there are other lives and opportunities."

Stan looked irritated. "Sure. But damn few that will pay you what we will."

"I don't need money," she said, and thought of Glenda Griffith. Ira could be with the Griffiths.... Not that she needed to know. That was over.

"I don't, either," Stan said unexpectedly. "But what else is there to do but make more?"

She laughed once more and started the engine. "I'll send you a list in a year or so, Stan. Goodbye and good luck."

At the house, Diane made a little ceremony out of giving a copy of her recently written will to Alycides, who turned pale with emotion.

"God willing, *hija*, Luz and I will never see you dead! We will be gone many years before...."

"I'm not planning to die, Aly. But if something happens to me, this paper is important. Remember the life estate for all of you old servants? It's in here." There was also a trust fund, to take the place of their salaries, but she didn't bother to mention that. All Alycides worried about was losing the home.

"Stay here! Here it is safe. There is danger in traveling to other places."

"I need to find my own place, Alycides."

THE NEXT MORNING Diane decided to buy new summer clothes before she did anything else. Driving across the bridge, she headed south, trying to make up her mind whether to shop on the fashionable boulevard known as Miracle Mile or at The Falls, a specialty, outdoor mall with landscaped walkways, wooden bridges and waterfalls. She ended up at neither; she turned off, without conscious decision, as soon as she came to the street that led to the Biscay Yacht Basin.

Big John was hosing down the docks. She saw him frown as she stepped out of her car and started toward him. Frowning, he turned off the spigot and waited, his water-splattered shorts clinging to his heavy body, his bare feet grateful for the puddles on hot concrete.

"If you're looking for Nicholson," he growled as she came up, "he ain't here."

She stopped, looking at him calmly. "I know. I came to ask you if you knew where he went."

Big John shifted his feet. "He goes where he wants to go, once he gets started. Anyway, he sure didn't tell me to pass on any information."

Feeling vibration on the dock, Diane looked around and saw Rosie Thomas coming toward them. The expression on Rosie's round face was as baleful as Big John's.

"Well, if it isn't Miss Don't-Call-Me, I'll-Call-You," Rosie said, apparently to Big John. "What does she want?"

Big John spat into the water. "Wants to know where Ira went."

"Don't tell her!"

"I ain't."

Caught between them, Diane looked from one to the other. "Will one of you tell me what's wrong?"

Rosie widened her stance, put her hands onto her hips and jutted her chin. "There's not a chance in the world that you don't already know."

"I don't already know."

"Come on. Your new guy was down here, telling Ira he was taking you over. You really know how to hurt a guy, babe. Couldn't you find the time to tell him yourself?"

"But . . . that's not true! I don't have a—a new guy. Besides, there was never anything . . . anything between Ira and me. Really there wasn't."

"There was, too!" Rosie almost spat out the words, staring at her venomously. "There was plenty between you!"

Diane shut her eyes for a moment, then opened them again, her face pale. "There wasn't supposed to be. I'll leave," she added, "if you'll let me by."

"Wait a minute," Big John said from behind her. "What do you want from Nicholson, anyway?"

She turned and faced the huge, glowering man once again. There were probably a thousand answers for that, but nothing she was sure of; nothing anyone else had a right to know. She straightened, her courage coming back. "Why should I tell you? You haven't done me any favors. I'll find him anyway, without your help." She whirled and strode toward shore, ignoring Rosie, who scrambled to get out of her way.

The next day, Diane flew to Governor's Harbour, rented a car and drove to the beach house. On the way she checked the yachts lying at anchor; the *Sea Fever* was not among them. Her heart sank, but she went on, hoping the Griffiths would know where Ira was.

Glenda was home alone and delighted to see her. She practically dragged her into the house. "I suppose Ira's gone fishing, too," she said, "like Don Mueller and Jack. I'm so glad you came over! If nothing else, we can pass the time on the skeet range...."

It took time to wait out Glenda's outpouring and explain, but Diane didn't mind. The warm welcome eased the chill she'd gotten at Biscay Yacht Basin. Watching Glenda take the news, Diane saw the real concern in her eyes.

"That's bad, Di. Jack and I have known Ira for a lot of years, and we've never seen him act like a man in love until he brought you around. He must be terribly hurt."

Diane paced back and forth in the huge Florida room. "I was a fool. I should have let him know what was going on, what I was doing. I —I thought he would be bored by it, so I didn't. But the main problem is Stanton Rogers. He lied." She stopped, thinking back. "No. He didn't. He asked me about Ira, and I said we were through. I said it was in the past." She turned and looked at Glenda, tears in her eyes. "I was afraid to hope, afraid it really was over, and maybe it is now. But I've got to find out."

"First," Glenda said practically, "we've got to find Ira. Let me do some calling. Let's see—Don and Jack will be either on Chub Cay or over at Bimini. They'll be in by now, and they may know something. Anyway, all the yachtsmen know Ira and they can ask around." She headed for the telephone.

It turned out that Don and Jack were in Bimini, a crossroads stop for yachts both going to and coming from the Bahamas and the Caribbean islands. Endless talk about weather, about mutual friends and acquaintances, went on around the Bimini docks and in the bars.

"Jack is bound to find out something," Glenda reassured Diane as she served the meal she had hastily put together. "If Ira's anywhere from here to Grenada, someone will have seen him. Or seen his boat. Or heard about him. All we have to do is wait."

The wait was long. It was past midnight when Don Mueller called, his voice fogged by alcohol.

"Got it, Glen'a. Ol' Roy Farley saw Ira three days ago in P.R. Said he was on his way to—to Charlotte Amalie. Goin' down to play with the Texans, he said." He laughed hoarsely. "You got me drunk, Glen'a, keeping me in this bar. . . . Ol' Jack is snug in bed."

Glenda was smiling widely, looking at Diane. "Okay, Don. You did fine. Thank you! Now, go snug down yourself, friend." Hanging up, she turned to Diane. "That's it. Seen in Puerto Rico and on his way to Charlotte Amalie. Go back to Miami and fly to Saint Thomas. Then look up the Texans."

"The Texans?"

"There's been an exodus of Texans to Saint Thomas Island. That island belongs to the U.S. Virgins, and there's dozens of Texans living down there now. Just ask, anyone will tell you where they hang out. Charlotte Amalie is gorgeous, you'll love it. And it's a small town, you may have to look at a lot of boats, but you'll find the *Sea Fever*. It's bound to be in the Charlotte Amalie harbor."

"Fine," Diane said calmly. She'd manage. She'd find him somehow. He might be gone again, but someone would remember him. He was easy to remember and hard to forget. In any case, she was going to follow every lead until she found him. "Then that's settled. When's the next flight out?"

"Relax. Not until tomorrow noon."

"Oh. How far is it?"

"To Charlotte Amalie? I don't know exactly. But it has to be around a thousand miles from Miami."

"Oh," Diane said again and sat down. *A thousand miles.* Ira must have been making sure he wouldn't see her again, to put that much space between them. "I don't suppose," she said slowly, "that Don's informant knew whether Ira was alone . . . or had someone with him."

"He'd be alone," Glenda said quickly. "I'm sure of it."

Diane stared at her. There was no way Glenda could know that unless the informant had said so, and obviously he hadn't. But it didn't matter. She'd go, anyway.

LATE FRIDAY AFTERNOON Diane watched from a scratched and dim window of a Boeing 747 as the plane dropped toward an island set in the turquoise waters of the Caribbean Sea. She hadn't expected the green hills, the sharp slopes, the beauty of Charlotte Amalie Harbor, a huge, half-landlocked bowl of deep, clear water. Three immense cruise ships lay along one side. A perfect advertisement, she thought, for the Getaway vacation. Glancing back as the plane turned and dropped lower, she saw that besides the crowded docks and shores, the surface of the harbor was speckled with yachts, sailboats, other craft. Glenda was right; she was going to have to look at a lot of boats before she found the *Sea Fever*.

At the airport she rented a car and drove to the hotel where her travel agent had reserved a room. Once settled in, she went down to the airy, beautifully decorated

lobby and asked the clerk for directions to the most
popular marinas.

"I'm looking for a large yacht," she ended, hoping for
the off chance of a miracle, "named the *Sea Fever*. I don't
suppose you've ever heard of it?"

The clerk, a red-faced, amiable man, grinned. "Why,
sure I have, ma'am." The Texas accent was rich and pure.
"That's Nicholson's boat. One of the fastest around. But
he doesn't keep it in a marina. It's anchored out."

Diane let out a breath and took one in, deeply, pushing down an impulse to grab the man and shake more
information loose. "That's amazing," she said, trying to
take her time. "You're the first person I've asked. Can you
tell me where Mr. Nicholson is staying?"

"Sure can! That's real easy. He's staying here." He
turned away to answer a ringing phone, talked for interminable seconds, hung up and checked the room keys in
their slots. "Nicholson's not in now, but I expect he'll be
at the warm-up barbecue this evening. You can catch him
there."

Diane had regained control of herself and accepted the
miracle with gratitude. "Great. Will you tell me where
the, ah, warm-up barbecue will be?"

The clerk looked pleased. "Sure. The barbecue's always at The Dallas Pit Stop, down near the shore. It's
only a coupla blocks from here, straight toward the water and turn right. You want to be there around eight,
eight-thirty, after the first coupla rounds of beer. When
you get close you'll hear it. All the Texans will be there,
including yours truly."

Diane thanked him and left, heading for the elevator
on shaky legs. All at once she was scared, wondering if
she might be making a fool of herself. Maybe Ira was glad
to be free. All she had to go on was what that mad little

woman at the Biscay Yacht Basin had said . . . *You really know how to hurt a guy.* Maybe that woman was just exaggerating. Maybe he wasn't hurt at all. It would be awful if he didn't want her around. She left the elevator and went briskly into her room, shut the door and sat down on the edge of the bed, more frightened than she'd ever been. Maybe she should simply forget this and go home. If Ira really wanted her, he'd come back.

Or would he? She sighed, kicked off her shoes, swiveled around on the bed and lay back, staring up at the ceiling and thinking of Yuri Stephan. *I want you to take a chance*, Yuri had said. *Promise to try.* Had Yuri known that she lacked the courage to try, when the possibilities included failure? Ira had taught her to believe in herself, win or lose. Only this time she didn't know if she could stand losing.

At seven-thirty she forced herself up from the bed and took a shower. She dressed with care in a white lace, sleeveless low-cut top that clung to the swell of her breasts, the taut line of her narrow waist. The white silk skirt, bias cut, hugged her hips and swirled around her knees. She let her sable hair swing loose and free, studied herself in the mirror and decided she looked daring, which proved appearances could lie. It was eight o'clock and she was still scared.

The Dallas Pit Stop was easy to find. She walked briskly down the well-lighted streets, feeling the cool air breathing in from the sea and listening to her frightened heart pounding in her ears. The last half block she had only to follow a bellowing chorus of "The Rose of San Antone." The Pit Stop was a typical, family-type restaurant and bar, filled with Texans of all ages, right down to newborns. She didn't find Ira. She was still looking, hesitating at each row of tables and booths, straining her eyes in the dim lights, peering into dark corners, when a man rose from a nearby table and came to her.

"Remember me, Miss Roberts? I'm from the hotel. Nicholson isn't here yet. Want to come sit with my wife and me?"

"That's very kind of you," Diane said stiffly, "but I'll take a table alone. After all, he may not show."

"Okay. There's a table for two back there against the wall. Better grab it while you can. I'll keep an eye out for Nicholson."

"Thank you. Thank you very much." She was trembling again, conscious of everyone's eyes on her. A stranger, she thought, in a strange land. A tropical island annexed by Texans was definitely strange. She walked back to the empty table, aware of the muted whistles and soft remarks. There were few single men in the crowd, but those few were clearly interested. They were all staring. She sat down and stared at the menu, at her hands.

"Care to order, miss?"

She looked up, seeing the bright, inquisitive face of a middle-aged waitress, a pad in her hand, a pencil poised.

"Yes, please," Diane said rapidly. "A—a martini. No, make that a daiquiri."

"Strawberry?"

"What?" A tall, familiar figure was coming in, a dark silhouette against the entrance lights, going toward the bar. "What? Oh, strawberry. No. Just . . . just a plain daiquiri. Please." The hotel clerk had gotten up and gone to the bar, leaning on it, talking. Shaggy, brown- and gold-streaked hair shone in the light as Ira bent to listen. Then the hotel clerk gestured toward the back wall and Diane held her breath, watching Ira's head jerk up, his face turn toward her. Even in the dim light she could have sworn she saw the golden gleam of his tiger eyes. Then he came striding toward her, ignoring the greetings of friends, weaving between the tables like a halfback on a football field. He slid into the chair opposite her and took her hands into his in one fluid motion.

"Sparrow," he said, and drew in a long breath. "I don't believe this. How did you happen to come here?"

He was glad to see her. That made all the difference in the world. "I came to find you," she said. "I . . . was lonely."

He smiled and held her hands to his face, kissing one palm and then the other, breathing in her fragrance. He had a million questions, but was afraid to ask even one. "I need you, Sparrow. Stay with me."

"I need you, too. That's why I came."

"Let's get out of here."

She nodded and rose, then stopped. "I ordered a daiquiri, Ira . . . wait." She fumbled with her purse and he pushed it away, taking a bill from his pocket and dropping it onto the table. "There. That'll take care of it."

Diane laughed softly, as he led her through the tables. "I'll say. It'll make her evening. That was a fifty." She glanced over to where the hotel clerk sat with his wife and saw him staring at them, obviously fascinated. She smiled brightly and waved. He waved back, grinning widely, and turned to whisper to his wife.

"Nice people," Diane said, her heart full, running over. "Friendly."

Ira put an arm around her as they stepped outside. "Anyone would be friendly to you." He sounded gruff, emotional. "But we couldn't stay there. They're all people I know. I'd be explaining you all evening." He looked down at her. "I want to be alone with you."

"I want that, too."

They were nearly at the hotel when Ira asked her if she was hungry.

"Not really," Diane said. "I had a huge lunch on the plane. But if you are, I'll eat something."

He shook his head, taking her arm as they went up the steps. "I'm not. Anyway, there's always room service." His eyes flicked down to hers as he opened the door. "Your place or mine?"

Memories flooded in. Good memories. "What floor are you on?"

His brows shot up, questioning. "The second floor."

"Yours, then. I'm on the third. That's too long to wait."

They laughed, holding hands in the elevator, and then, inside his room, looked at each other and fell silent. He took her into his arms and held her, his cheek against her hair. She burrowed, conscious of his familiar, sensual odor, of the crisp hair in the V of his open shirt, the warmth of his skin. The back of her throat ached, her eyes filled with tears. "Darling," she whispered, "my darling Ira. I thought I'd lost you."

His arms tightened, she felt the deep vibration of his voice against her breasts. "I thought you'd found someone else. I felt like a fool for sending Stan to you."

"Shh." She was slowly unbuttoning his shirt, pushing it away, touching his chest with her fingertips, smoothing the crisp hair. "There's no one else..." She slipped her hands inside the opened shirt and looked up. Dark eyes met hers and probed deeply.

"You told Stan we were through. I know you did. Stan's never been a liar. I told myself not to care—that we'd never planned for a future together. But I wanted to kill him. I wanted it so badly I was afraid to stay there, where I might see you together."

She dropped her forehead against his shoulder and nodded. "I did say that.... I was afraid to hope for more. It—it was a bad time for me. I wanted you so desperately, but I kept remembering what we'd said. You know, the cruise was supposed to be just a—a fun thing. An adventure."

"A lifetime with you would still be an adventure, Sparrow." His voice was soft and shaky warm, his hands cupped her face and raised it, his golden eyes burned with desire. "Kiss me," he whispered. "Make love to me. Make me believe you want me. I need to know, to really know...."

Could she? She wanted to. Oh, she wanted to. She could feel herself responding, her breasts tightening, a liquid fire running through her veins, a demand inside her she couldn't resist. Diane moved, lowering her eyes from his. Pressing her face against his neck, she took a deep breath and wondered how to start. But... but he had always led, he was so skilled, so adept.... What if she did something stupid, awkward, laughable? She'd lose...she'd spoil their reunion. He'd be sorry he'd asked.

"Don't," Ira breathed, sensing her thoughts. "Don't be afraid to try."

She nodded, once. Something Ira did was undress her, and it always excited her. She could do that. She began to take off his clothes, her face flushed and intent as she tossed his shirt aside, her hands shaking and then gentling, smoothing and kneading his muscular back, sliding down to his waist. Then she stepped back and looked, seeing that he was already aroused. She smiled, looking up at him provocatively, feeling much surer of herself. It was working, but he was holding back, still making her take the lead. She thought of the second time they'd kissed, and why he had lost control. She began to breathe faster. But she knew what she wanted to do.

The trousers he wore were a thin, silk blend, smooth as satin, and fitted him beautifully. They were a joy to touch, to caress and feel the warmth of him beneath. She moved close, running her hands over him, feeling the hardness, the size, remembering how well they fitted together. Then, answering the ache in her own loins, she pressed herself sinuously against him, slipped her arms around his waist and cupped his hard buttocks with her palms. He was hot, hot as fire through the thin silk. She held him tight, rocked against him, feeling her own hot liquid pooling deep inside, leaning back with parted lips and closed eyes, breathless with her own rising passion.

"Diane! I'm...I can't...it's been too long." Ira's voice was strangled, hoarse, insistent. She opened her eyes as his arms went around her and jerked her against him full length. His mouth covered hers in a drugging kiss, his hands explored her feverishly. Breathing hard, he picked her up and strode to the bed. In minutes he had them both naked and fitted together; one vibrating, passionate organism with two racing hearts, tossing in a storm of violent emotion, climaxing in a rolling, thunderous ecstasy that left them both struggling for breath. But as they drifted back to reality, Ira refused to move away from her.

"Just wait," he said, easing his weight onto his elbows. "Let me stay. That was my fault."

"Fault?" She smiled contentedly, brushing back the gold-streaked hair that fell over his forehead. "What fault?"

"Too fast. I shouldn't have asked you to make love to me. I only have to look at you to get raunchy. You're a wonderful lover, though. I nearly went crazy." He moved, settling deeper, and kissed her again. "Mmm, good. How I've missed you, Sparrow. How I wanted you . . . how I still want you. Oh, darling, how I'll always, always want you."

She was silent, amazed, lying there and feeling his passion return. He was growing inside her, hardening, pressing insistently, and then she was gasping in wonder, for all at once her flesh answered his with a swelling warmth, an eager welcome. She heard her own low moans of desire, and then her arms were tightening, her hips tilting, her slender legs twining around his thighs. Swinging into his rhythmic movement, she gave herself over to his slow, delicious lovemaking.

16

A WEEK LATER, in the midmorning of a calm day, the *Sea Fever* moved sedately through the crowded harbor, rounded Hassel Island and entered the Caribbean Sea. Ira swung her west by northwest and headed her around Saint Thomas toward the Atlantic and Puerto Rico. He eased the throttles forward when they cleared the last boat coming in, and took off, raising a cloud of glittering foam. He grinned at Diane and shrugged.

"I can't resist a little of her speed, even though we're going only sixty or seventy miles today. We'll spend the night at San Juan and buy diesel fuel. I'm filling all the tanks, so we'll have enough for two thousand miles. That's nearly twice as much as we need."

Tanned, contented and relaxed, Diane grinned back at him. "Sounds like a great safety margin. Where are we going, then?"

"Anywhere and everywhere you want. The next month is ours, unless a hurricane blows in. After that we'll do some serious thinking about the future."

She was still smiling, but looked away. During the past week—a week of lovemaking, of laughter, of experiences she knew she'd treasure the rest of her life—Ira had talked about the future. He wanted to use his hunting skills, but in a completely different way than he had formerly.

"They need me," he had said, discussing the dedicated men and women trying to save endangered species. "They can't help the animals, can't study what they eat, when they mate and when they give birth, if they can't find them. I'd be useful there. Think about it, Sparrow."

Diane hadn't answered him then and let it drop now. She had no problem deciding whether she'd like to go or not; she knew she would. She knew now that she was in love with Ira. Totally. Head over heels, or was it heart over head? If Ira asked for commitment, for a promise to stay with him, so that they would belong only to each other, she would agree. The trouble was: he hadn't asked. In a moment she climbed out of the chair, stretched mightily and yawned.

"Any requests for food or drink?"

He looked up at her, his strange eyes softening. She glowed with that tan, with that look of contentment. The scar on her forehead was more noticeable now, pale against the tanned skin. She had said recently that she might have someone look at it, maybe fix it, and fix her nose at the same time.

"I don't need them anymore," she'd added. "I don't need to remember that sad, stupid affair."

He had been warmed by knowing he'd helped to erase her fears, to lower her defenses against life. He put a hand on her waist, sliding it under her loose blouse and caressing the smooth skin. Watching her smile, seeing her blue eyes darken, he felt a leap of desire, a hot stirring in his loins.

"I'm only hungry for you, darling. Just come up once in a while and shake me out of my dreams."

She smiled and left him, going into the galley to wash up the breakfast dishes and cups. They had moved onto the boat yesterday to make ready for the trip, and she'd practiced her budding cooking skills again, making a simple dinner last night and breakfast this morning. It had been fun, and Ira had helped her. Now, washing up, she reminded herself that nothing lasted forever, and the best way to handle the end was to make the most of everything good. If, when the time came for Ira to leave for Alaska, he still wanted her to go, she'd go—if *she* wanted to. There wasn't much doubt in her mind that she'd want to, but to be absolutely fair and impartial—

"I'm thirsty!" Ira roared. "Stop ignoring me!"

She jumped, laughed and opened the refrigerator, taking out the orange juice.

THEY LEFT SAN JUAN before dawn the next morning. Ira had thought of a place he wanted Diane to see.

"Grand Turk, on Turks Island," he had said at dinner the night before. "We'll make it tomorrow if we've a calm sea to run, but probably after dark. It's a long way from here. But it's absolutely the best place for diving. Reefs you won't believe. The island is nothing but scrub and sand, no tourist traps, no fancy hotels. But you'll like it."

Excited, Diane laughed. "I know I will! Any dragons?"

"Probably. They travel as stowaways on most boats, and they seem to live everywhere on the islands. That's probably all we'll find—dragons and divers."

Out of the blue, Diane's chest tightened with premonition. She wondered why, and thought of the last diving they'd done. "No sharks?"

"No guarantees. That's like asking if some wild driver is going to slam into you on a turnpike. It's always possible, but not likely."

Now, leaving the coast of Puerto Rico, heading north into a sloppy sea and a freshening, westerly breeze, Ira wasn't as cheerful. Going to Turks Island no longer seemed like a great idea. As the sky lightened toward dawn he saw low, tattered clouds, gray instead of white, racing to the east.

"Squalls," he told Diane. "Maybe the weather will change, but it could blow harder." He glanced over at her still, calm face and with the intuition of a lover, guessed how she felt. When she looked that quiet, she was worried or uncertain. "It won't be dangerous," he added offhandedly, "just slow and uncomfortable. The *Sea Fever* is as seaworthy as they come. She can handle a gale."

She relaxed and smiled, leaning back. "Who could complain about one bumpy ride? We've been amazingly lucky until now. I wasn't really worrying about the weather, anyway. I trust you on that." She hadn't been worrying about the squalls. She'd been wondering if she was becoming clairvoyant. That feeling of premonition last evening had been strong. It was still nagging at the edge of her thoughts.

The weather worsened as the day dragged on. The squalls came, with hard, driving rain that drummed against the hastily closed, sliding windows of the wheelhouse. Ira became increasingly silent, watching the radar closely so he could avoid other craft, constantly checking his course on the loran. In midafternoon the rain stopped, but the wind picked up and blew from the north. The seas rose, battering against the bow of the yacht, slowing it down. Ira cursed and set a lower speed. The yacht pushed on, seawater and foam flying against the windshields.

"That settles it, Sparrow. We'll not make Turks Island tonight. But we'll make Mouchair Bank by dark, and try anchoring there in the lee of one of the sandbars. We'll have only fifty or sixty miles more to run tomorrow."

"Sounds fine." She settled deeper into her chair, watching the angry sea and the dark blot of a small, ragged-looking ship coming toward them. Minutes ago the ship had been no more than a blip on the radar screen, but the wind was helping it move along at a fair rate of speed. It was one of the very few vessels they'd seen today, and she started to point it out to Ira. Then she saw that he was already watching it. Watching and frowning.

"Listen," he said suddenly. "Get a couple of those military rifles out and load them, will you? If the captain of that freighter has any wrong ideas, I want him to know we can protect ourselves. We're moving into the worst of the drug-smuggler territory."

Diane's eyes widened, and then she was gone, half running, half staggering toward the saloon as the yacht bucked against the waves. Grabbing the wood rosette on the couch, she twisted it, and the drawer slid open, displaying its cargo of oiled and gleaming weapons. She removed two of the automatic rifles, laying them side by side on the rug, and loaded them swiftly, her hands steady and sure as she slammed in the cartridge magazines. Then, rising, she carried them both forward, through the galley and to the door of the wheelhouse. Ira glanced around.

"That was quick. Put one there, just inside the door, and take the other to the aft deck—no, just inside at that door, too. That could be handy in case of attack. Brace them so they won't slide around, and then come back here."

She did as she was told, anchoring both rifles with heavy cushions from the couch, watching them a moment to be certain they wouldn't slide on the rocking decks. Then she went back to her chair and saw that the freighter was slowing, turning closer to their path. In a moment a blaze-orange flag blossomed on a slim pole above the freighter's wheelhouse and a man stepped out, waving his arms. Ira made a sound of disgust, slowed the *Sea Fever* and stood up.

"Would you look at that? Coming down the sea-lane on full power and then running up a distress flag to coax us over. He must really think he's found a sucker. Take the wheel, Diane." He watched her slide into his seat and put her shaky hands onto the wheel. "Just keep her headed into the waves and you'll do fine. I won't be a minute."

Diane froze to the wheel as he stepped away, felt it turn and turned it back, slow and easy, afraid to look around. She knew what he was doing—he was picking up that loaded gun. But she didn't know what he would do with it. When she heard him slide open the door and step out, she looked around. The freighter was creeping closer, but it was still too faraway to see the man's face clearly. Surely Ira wouldn't...? She gasped, seeing him raise the rifle to his shoulder on the rocking deck, take careful aim and fire.

"Got it!" Ira's voice was triumphant, amused.

Diane stared. The blaze-orange flag was gone; it showed for a moment on the top of a tossing wave and was gone again. The pole that held it was splintered in two. The man had quit waving and run back into the wheelhouse. An instant later the freighter puffed out a black cloud of smoke and left, heading south again at a smart pace. Ira stepped back inside, grinning. "For a pirate," he said, "he's uncommonly timid."

"That pole," Diane said, her voice still wavering from fright, "was rocking back and forth, and so were you! Don't you dare tell me that shot wasn't luck!"

"I wouldn't think of it." He leaned over her and kissed her hard, grabbing the wheel as it started to turn. "Now, if you'll give me my seat again, we'll get there sooner. Frankly, I feel better than I have all day."

She moved to her own seat, holding on because her legs were weak, and because, when he increased the speed, the yacht's movement was even rougher. She sat down, still staring at him. "It was, wasn't it? Luck, I mean."

"Oh, sure. With a shot like that, there's always a little luck."

But he'd known he could do it. She settled back, watching the monotonous slop of foam and water across the windshield. "So," she said wryly, "that's why you never joined in at skeet. You didn't want to show me up."

He glanced over. "It's impossible to show up a person who keeps getting perfect scores."

"But you would have done it with a rifle."

"Maybe. Maybe not. I've missed, plenty of times. You ought to try a rifle for skeet, darling. You're plenty good enough, and it puts the fun back in."

"No! I'd miss, and everyone would laugh."

"What's so bad about that? Your friends might laugh, but they'd still love you just as much."

"Just as much?" She was still wry. "Now that may be true. Except for Alycides and Luz, who wouldn't care if I missed, I can't think of anyone who loves me."

"I do."

She stared again at the sloshing water and foam and damned herself for saying what she had said; damned him for treating it lightly. She felt hot with embarrassment and yet tired of trying to hide her feelings. She slid from the chair, not looking at him. "I think," she said carefully, "I ought to go lie down for a while. If you need anything, yell. I'll be on the couch."

THEY WERE ANCHORED in the lee of a large, sloping sand-bar near the deep Mouchair Passage before either of them spoke again. They'd made it as the gray twilight slipped away in what seemed like minutes and became a black night, with a sky offering only a glimpse now and then of stars shining through slowly drifting clouds. Stepping out onto the aft deck as the yacht came tight on the anchor line, Diane decided there was a moon up there somewhere, for one area in the eastern sky sported a dim, circular glow. There was also one saving grace—the wind had dropped to no more than a ten-knot breeze and the seas were near normal. Relieved, though still hurt by what she felt was Ira's callous remark, Diane went back inside to turn on the lights and start dinner. She could move around in the galley with no trouble now; she was used to the gentle heave and swing. She looked up as Ira came in and broke the silence.

"I defrosted steaks," she said, carefully polite. "After a day like this, I think we need something solid."

He stood looking at her, his bronzed face nearly expressionless. "Fine. When do you want to eat?"

She gazed at him in surprise. "Why... a half hour, maybe a few minutes more."

"Fine," he repeated. "I'll have time for a shower." He left, ignoring the wine she'd poured for him, disappearing down the companionway without another word. She turned away, her throat constricting. For the first time he'd shut her out. No, he'd moved out—out of their circle of easy familiarity, of companionship, of shared humor, shared thoughts. He was angry with her and she didn't know why. Something had gone wrong, really wrong, since she'd left him sitting there in the wheel-house.

Going ahead with the salad, scoring the fat on the steaks, she thought he must have guessed she'd taken offense at his kidding around about love. Looking back upon it, she wondered herself why she'd taken it so hard. The words had hurt, but he hadn't meant them to hurt. He had no idea that she was hopelessly in love with him. In fact, she thought heavily, slapping the steaks onto the hot griddle, it might have been the famous, last straw. He was probably damn well tired of her constant, stupid sensitivity!

She stared at the thick steaks, trying to judge when to turn them over, while her mind argued on and on. She could have told him how she felt, and he would have understood. Except if he knew she loved him, he'd get out of her life as gracefully as he could. She wasn't ready to lose him. Would she ever be?

She was putting the food onto the table when Ira came up, wearing shorts and nothing else. He still ignored the wine, and sat down without comment to eat the steak and salad. They ate in heavy silence, while Diane racked her brain for something to say. When Ira finished his meal and stood up, she blurted out exactly what she was thinking.

"I'm sorry, Ira. It was stupid of me to take offense at what you said."

He was quiet, looking at her with the same reserve he'd shown earlier. "I'm sorry, too. I shouldn't have said it— at least, I shouldn't have said it in that way. It just came out. Let's forget it."

Diane smiled with relief and rose, reaching for him and winding her arms around his neck. "Yes. I promise you,

I'm going to stop being childish and learn to take your teasing."

"Teasing?" Ira grasped her arms and pulled them away from his neck, staring at her. "I wasn't teasing you, Sparrow. Don't make a fool of me by pretending I didn't mean it."

"Pretending? I wasn't.... Are you saying you were serious?"

"Hell, yes! I'm sorry! I know I wasn't supposed to get serious. I know what you'd think if I asked you to marry me, so I won't. But I can't stop loving you. I've tried, but it's the keeper kind—all the way, for all the lifetime left to me. It was just a damn dumb way to bring it up."

"Oh, Ira . . ." She was laughing, half crying. "That's wonderful! I'm so in love with you . . . I never dreamed . . ."

He was looking at her with such open love that she could hardly speak, but then in the next instant his face had grown hard, stiff, and he'd grabbed her into his arms, cutting off her breath, sliding a hand over her mouth.

"Shhh! I hear an engine, the wrong kind. Let's get these lights out!"

"Oh, *no!*" She put a hand over her mouth, hearing the sound now, watching him leap toward the light switches beside the open door. His hand was on them when the first shot cracked, and the weight of his falling body dragged the hand down, turning the lights out, the cabin black.

"Ira! No, please . . ." She stumbled through darkness, conscious of the sound coming nearer, the rumbling growl of a high-powered engine. Her shocked mind babbled words. Wrong kind . . . wrong time of night . . . smugglers. They'd killed him; they would kill her, too. She knelt, touching him, feeling his face, running her hands over his head. He was still, too still, and there was a sticky mess in his thick hair. "Ira," she whispered, "Ira." They could kill her now.... She wouldn't care.... He was gone.

There were faint voices out there. For a moment a light came on, then blinked out. Under her hands Ira moved, jerked convulsively. *He wasn't dead.* But he was helpless, and they were right there. Diane stepped over Ira and found the rifle by the wheelhouse door. She picked it up and stepped out, looking through the open window. She could hear the rumble getting closer, hear the slosh and slap of water, and in a moment she made out the shape of the long, low boat. A speedboat, one of the Cigarette type. She saw a dim shape in the bow, saw the flash of teeth as he laughed. Laughed. She felt anger leap up, pushing aside shock.

She raised the rifle she held and looked through the night scope. The man sprang to life, magnified, his figure limned in a dim, red glow, even his features recognizable. She was shaking, thinking of taking a human life, wondering if she could. He spoke. The sound carried clearly across the water.

"Hell, I got him, or he'd be shooting now. That woman'll be too scared to do anything. Let's get it!"

Diane zeroed in on his chest and pulled the trigger. The boat roared into a fast turn, throwing the man out as he fell. There were two more men in the middle of the boat, and as they slowed, looking for the one she'd shot, she found the back of one of them in her scope and fired again. He shrieked, a long, eerie, agonized wail that shuddered through the black night and made her skin crawl. The boat was gone, the roar of the engine receding in the distance. Behind her Ira groaned and sat up.

"Diane! Where are you?"

"Here." She went to him swiftly and knelt in the darkness, touching him. "Be still," she said as he tried to get up. "You've been hurt. I chased them away. They've got one of those fast boats."

"I heard it. Help me up."

"Wait till I turn on the lights."

"No! They'll be back. Don't give them a target."

She gulped and swallowed, suddenly nauseated. "There's only one of them left, Ira. I—I think I killed the other two. Maybe the one will give up."

Ira was silent for a moment. She could feel him staring at her in the darkness. "I'm sorry," he said finally. "I know it's a shock. But they would have killed you and finished me off. You did what you had to do. Now help me get to the radio. Those boats travel in pairs, sometimes more."

"Please," she said, "don't get up. I'll do whatever needs to be done. You aren't just hurt, Ira. You've been shot in the head. You may have a bullet in there, and I d-d-don't want you to d-d-die." She leaned forward and sobbed, arms around him, holding him tight while she fought for control. Wiping her eyes, she said, "Just tell me what to do first."

Ira shook his head, then grabbed it with both hands, cursing under his breath, searching with his fingers for the wound, letting out his breath as he found it. "It's all right. The wound has stopped bleeding and the bullet didn't penetrate. It knocked me out, I'm dizzy, and my head aches like hell, but I'm not going to die. However, I am going to get up. I've got to call the U.S. Coast Guard."

She helped him to the radio in the wheelhouse, gave him the rifle she'd been using and listened to his directions. He told her to go aft and watch for anything coming up behind them. He reminded her that there was a rifle at the saloon door.

"Don't expose yourself to their guns," he said. "They'll be aware of resistance now and angry. They may sweep the decks with automatic fire. They do that to terrorize, to make deals with frightened people and then kill them. But you can see a target a hell of a lot better than they can. Don't hesitate—shoot them. We're on our own."

"What about the U.S. Coast Guard?"

"They'll come. In a cutter if one is close enough, or in a plane. But it takes time, and we haven't any."

Diane nodded and left, stopping to feel around in the drawer for more ammunition. She took a full magazine back to Ira and kept one with her. She picked up the rifle, then stood leaning against the door, watching the dark, heaving sea and listening to Ira talk on the radio. The call seemed to require an immense amount of detailed information about the *Sea Fever*: length, color, tonnage, power, documentation. About the position, loran readings, depth of water, nearest land. They also asked whom else to notify. Next of kin? She moved restlessly, catching a different sound. Then she turned and yelled through the open door.

"They're coming, Ira! Sounds like a heavy engine, wide open!" She heard the microphone clatter as he dropped it.

"All right! I'm ready. If they're coming fast, they'll have an Uzi sweeping the deck. Stay behind something solid. Maybe you'll get a shot at them after they pass, but don't do anything foolish."

"Right." She listened to the roaring engine speeding toward them and her mind raced to meet it. An Uzi. Nine-millimeter shells, deadly and fast, but they'd never penetrate the thick fiberglass of the *Sea Fever*. She was out, scrambling across the aft deck, crouching behind the foot-high, fiberglass coaming that held the chrome railing. She went flat, plastering herself on the deck as the speedboat suddenly materialized with a terrifying crackle of gunfire. Then she was sitting up, snapping the rifle to her shoulder, taking quick aim at a dim huddle in the disappearing boat. She squeezed off three shots before it was gone, saw it swerve and heard the echo of Ira's rifle shots following hers. She sat back, sure they'd hit at least one, maybe two of the men. She breathed deeply, listening.

"Diane!" Ira roared. "Dammit, say something!"

"I'm fine!" she yelled back. "You be careful! I hear another one coming!"

"Then watch both sides! The first one's coming back!"

She froze, then relaxed. They couldn't hit her from either side; the trajectory was wrong. Their guns were below the level of the deck; she'd have to stand up to be seen, to get hit. She watched and calculated. Coming back, the first boat stopped shooting as they passed on the far side; probably, she supposed, to reload. Their friends in the second boat roared by her with a constantly chattering gun, slowing down and concentrating on the main cabin, shattering windows. That gave her a chance and she took it, scoring two hits that sent the boat leaping off course, skidding crazily back and forth and slowing. Ira's rifle cracked and the boat stopped, started again and moved out fast, away from them and out of range. Listening, she figured they had turned again, following the other speedboat. She turned her head toward the open door into the saloon and yelled.

"Are you okay?"

"Okay." Ira's voice was hoarse; he sounded exhausted. She scrambled to her feet and ran. Stumbling through broken glass in the dark, she came into the wheelhouse and found him slumped in her chair, his head drooping, rifle across his thighs.

"Ira!"

"I'm all right. I got careless and took a shot in the leg, but it's not dangerous. It just bled a little."

The wind had stopped, the glow of the hidden moon was brighter, and she couldn't hear a sound in any direction. She took a chance and turned on a small light. He was bleeding, all right; the blood had run down and puddled on the deck. "Ira," she said faintly, "how do we stop it?"

"It has stopped. It won't start again unless I move. Turn out that damn light!"

"No. I'll hear them if they come back. Right now I'm going to make a tourniquet."

"I don't need it."

"You will."

"Those men . . ."

"Now, listen!" Diane was shaking, scared for him, angry. "Do you hear any engines? We've hit at least five men in these boats. They'd have to be crazy to make another run."

He nodded, agreeing. "I don't expect another run. I expect a trick, a change of pace. They don't care about losing men, it makes their shares bigger. We're sitting in a hell of a prize, and they want it bad. Do as I tell you, Sparrow."

She turned out the light. Then she went down into the total darkness below and found her purse by fumbling in a drawer. She found a pencil flashlight and went into the corridor. She took a sheet from the linen closet, turned off the tiny light and went back up to look for a knife.

"Diane," Ira said quietly, "they're here."

She jumped and looked around, seeing nothing. She went into the wheelhouse. "Where?" She kept her shaking voice low.

"They're alongside. Listen. You'll hear a scrape, maybe a whisper. They went up tide, turned off their engines and drifted down, hoping we wouldn't see them. They'll probably try to board us in a rush, all at once, at the stern and up here at the same time. You'll have to shoot them as they come over the rail. Do you think you can handle that?"

Her heart beat painfully and tears came to her eyes. More killing. She reached out to him and felt his big hand clutch hers. He would die if they lost, and she would, too. That was what she had to remember. "We have to do it," she whispered. "We can't give up. We have to win." She put down the sheet and picked up her rifle and extra magazine, reloading. Avoiding the broken glass, she eased past the door and waited, then slung the gun up as she saw the first pair of hands rise stealthily from below and grasp the starboard railing.

When the man's head came into view, she shot him. And swung as a shot zipped past her. Her assailant was pulling himself up and over the rail on the other side. She shot him, and out of the corner of her eye saw the black silhouette of a third pair of hands to her left. She turned and waited, but the hands disappeared. She heard a thump, a curse and some scrambling, then the roar of an engine. One of the boats rocketed away, one man inside, bent low. Up at the bow Ira's rifle cracked, and a man's scream ended in a splash. Then there was silence. After a moment she spoke, her voice trembling.

"One man let go and ran away. I—I couldn't shoot him."

"That's fine." Ira's voice was faint, as if he spoke from the bottom of a well. "It's over, Sparrow. One man alone won't try us. Look on this side and you'll see the other boat drifting away, empty. We're safe...."

Diane went through the saloon, turning on lights, ignoring the mess, and turned on more lights in the galley, in the wheelhouse. Ira was lying back in her seat, his eyes closed and his bronzed face pale. His leg was dripping blood again and she hurried to cut the sheet, to fashion a rough imitation of a tourniquet. Then she didn't know where to put it, so she had to guess. When she started to tighten it, he opened his eyes.

"I'm all right. I don't need that. Just put on a pressure bandage and help me to the couch."

"Dammit, I don't know how!" she burst out.

"I'll tell you how, darling. Just listen..." He put out a hand and she took it, holding on tight. He smiled. "Don't you know yet that there's nothing we can't do together?"

Ira was bandaged and lying on the couch, sleeping peacefully, when the radio crackled out a curt, *"Sea Fever, Sea Fever,* this is the U.S. Coast Guard. Come in, *Sea Fever."*

Diane went into the wheelhouse and picked up the microphone. She wouldn't have wakened Ira for the president himself. And anyway, she'd listened enough to know how to answer. "This is the *Sea Fever,* answering a call from the U.S. Coast Guard. Go ahead, please."

"We have a message for Captain Nicholson, ma'am."

"You can give it to me. He's... busy."

"Yes, ma'am, I imagine he is. Well, you can tell him he'll have help by daybreak. There's a cutter on the way. Is everything under control so far?"

She was silent a moment, considering. Then she sighed. "Yes, sir. Everything's under control. We'll look forward to the help tomorrow."

"Good. Oh. Tell him we managed to find Mr. Griffith. He's flying to Grand Turk. He'll get someone to bring him to you."

"Fine." She hadn't known Ira had asked for Jack, but she was glad. "Uh, thanks for the call."

"Yes, ma'am. Glad to be of help."

Diane listened to the formal sign-off that followed, hooked up the mike and went back into the saloon. She cleaned up as well as she could and turned out the bright lights, leaving one small lamp so Ira could see if he woke. She was trying to find things to do, to keep her mind busy. Still she kept hearing that long, eerie wail of distress that had come shuddering through the night and made her skin crawl. She kept seeing the falling bodies and felt herself trembling with a deep sorrow.

"Diane."

She went to him quickly, bending down, touching him. He was too warm, his eyes glazed with fever but aware, looking at her.

"I'm all right," he said in answer to her worried look. "But you aren't. Your eyes are full of ghosts. I'm so sorry, Sparrow."

He knew how she felt about killing those men. About taking life. The knowledge was in his eyes, looking at her with love and understanding. She knelt by the couch and put her arms around him, her head upon his shoulder. She thought of the years they might have together, the things they might do that would make some small part of the world better. She thought of the bullet that came through the door, and the man outside on the dark sea, laughing. Bragging.

"It's all right," she said. "It was worth it. We're alive." She raised her head and kissed him. "The U.S. Coast Guard called. They'll be here in the morning. And so will Jack. He's flying into Grand Turk by dawn and planning on getting someone to bring him out to us."

"Great. Jack will take us to his place."

"Jack," Diane said very clearly, "will take us to our place—in Miami. I have an excellent doctor, and Luz is a wonderful cook. Now relax. You're hot with fever, and I'm going for aspirin and water. Then you must sleep."

Ira raised his brows. "Good Lord," he said. "I'm in love with a managing woman."

She kissed him again. "I know. It's wonderful. I found Yuri's kind of love, after all."

"You'll have to explain that to me."

She shook her head. "No. I'll live it with you, the rest of our lives."

Epilogue

"BARRING STORMS," Ira said lazily, "October is a lovely month in the Bahamas. Tomorrow begins the last week in September, and we haven't had a hurricane head this way yet. Let's go back to Norman's Cay."

He saw Diane's eyes light up, but she shook her head. "Not until we get married. We're not going anywhere, until you give in and propose to me."

It was late in the afternoon and they were lounging on the terrace of the old Stephan home, idly watching the tropical twilight creep through the huge oaks and shadow the long, sweeping stretches of green lawn. Ira glanced again at her and laughed.

"For a woman who said she would never marry, you're very persistent. Why? You know damn well that nobody could drag me away from you, so it isn't that."

"No, it isn't that." She looked away, her delicate profile still showing the small bump in her otherwise perfect nose, part of the jagged scar, a fan of long lashes, a corner of a smiling mouth. "It's—something else. Something I want, and I think you'll want. . . ." She glanced back at him. "If later you really hated it, we could get a divorce."

"What?"

"Don't yell. I just meant that if later you felt tied down. . . ."

"I like being tied down. I want to be tied down and I want you to be tied down. I just don't want to contemplate being married to Harrington Roberts's daughter. The man will have to die sometime. The idea of a billionairess wife is revolting."

She stared at him and got up. "I think it's high time you met my father. If you don't mind, I'll call and say we're coming for dinner."

"It won't change my mind," Ira warned.

Diane smiled. "Don't be too sure. My father can be very convincing—in his way." She left, going into the house and straight to the telephone.

Cora answered and they chatted for a while. Then, keeping it casual, Diane asked if she could bring a guest to dinner. "He's a very close friend," she added, "and I think he ought to meet my father."

"Oh!" Cora sounded startled. "So that's the way the wind blows. Why, Diane . . . I . . . well, I'm sure your father will be delighted to meet him."

"No, you're not."

Cora gave an embarrassed giggle. "That's true. Do you, uh, want me to tell him, or do you plan a surprise?"

"Suit yourself. He'll react the same way. Oh, do, please, call the guards at the gate and say I'm bringing a guest. My friend isn't the kind to put up with a body search."

"Will do, Di." Cora laughed again. "You know, I'm looking forward to this."

"So am I."

At seven that evening they drove through the gates of the Roberts compound and stopped. Forewarned by Cora, the uniformed guards checked the car's interior, nodded respectfully at Diane and stepped back. Driving on, Ira looked more amused than impressed.

"He has more guards than the president. How does he figure out how many he needs? One guard per million dollars?"

"Oh, heavens, no," Diane said with a straight face. "He doesn't have that many. He'd have to put up a barracks."

Ira grinned. He knew she was putting him on. "All right. So he's not as rich as Croesus. He's still too rich."

"He's poor," Diane said, suddenly serious. "Poor as a church mouse. You'll see."

Inside, the two uniformed guards watched Ira with more than the usual attention. Diane said nothing, knowing it was only Ira's size, his obviously fit physique, that worried them. Cora came to meet them, wearing her usual black skirt and white silk blouse, greeting them both warmly. Her eyes, skimming over Ira, were appreciative.

"Good luck," she said, pressing Diane's hand. "I've said only that you were bringing a guest."

Diane nodded, eyeing Cora affectionately. "Are you dining with us?"

"No." Cora smiled. "As usual when company comes, I've been given the evening off. Glad to have met you, Mr. Nicholson. Perhaps I'll see you again." She turned to Diane again. "He's in the library and impatient."

"Ah," Diane said, taking Ira's arm. "All the old family traditions. He's always in the library and he's always impatient. That's one of the things I like—you can count on him. Come on, Ira. Let's get this over with."

Harrington Roberts waited for them in his usual white suit, his small, petulant face drawn into tired, dissatisfied lines. He came forward as they entered and kissed Diane's cheek.

"What is this I hear about an attempt to kidnap you?" he asked and looked up at Ira. "Your fault, I suppose, taking her into a vulnerable area. You could have been killed, you know."

Diane sighed. "The men wanted the yacht, Father. Not me. If you read the story, you read what the U.S. Coast Guard reported. They were smugglers, not kidnappers."

"Don't you believe it. They were after my daughter." His eyes went to Ira, suspiciously. "It wouldn't have worked, you know. I wouldn't have given them a red cent."

"I'm hungry," Diane said quickly, "and thirsty. You're supposed to be entertaining us, Father, not arguing." She went to a tray on the library table, where a container of ice, seltzer and several glasses were grouped around decanters, and poured Scotch for all three of them. "There," she added, handing around the drinks. "Relax. The best is yet to come."

Ira looked at her curiously. She was exuberant, a look of pure devilry deep in her blue eyes. He was already beginning to understand why she had been so mixed-up; why she had taken so long to really believe in herself. And he wondered what she had planned.

The dinner was planned by Cora and it was delicious. It included lobster Bordelaise, and when he was served, Ira turned and looked at Diane.

"Coincidence?"

She shook her head. "Request. I wanted memories to taunt you."

Harrington, pushing food around his plate and consuming glass after glass of wine, watched them and glowered. They chatted; he waited. He looked more and more inquisitive as the evening wore on, and finally, as the dessert of cheese and fruit came in, he asked.

"I know you had some reason, Diane, for inviting yourself to dinner tonight. I'll tell you right now, if it's money you want, you won't get it from me. You're capable of working, so work. Why a daughter of mine ever wanted to grind in some office is beyond me, but you did, against my orders. So, do it again."

Diane smiled at him. "I don't need money, Father. I never will, thanks to Yuri. I came only to bring Ira here to meet you. I wanted you to know the man I'm going to marry."

"Marry? Ha!" Harrington turned and looked at Ira, who stared, first at Diane and then at Harrington Roberts. He started to speak, but Harrington cut him off.

"You'll not get a red cent, you—you gigolo! I bet you arranged that kidnapping attempt in the Bahamas yourself! I'm right, aren't I? When that didn't work, you decided to propose. Don't you think I'm smart enough to know you're just after my money?"

Ira was silent, staring again at Diane. She was composed, sipping her wine and listening to her father. But the look of devilry was still in her eyes. Slowly Ira relaxed and turned back to Harrington.

"I'm willing to wait," he said. "It might not be long, you know. Something could happen to you."

Harrington leaped to his feet. "Don't you threaten me, you fortune hunter. I'll cut Diane out of my will if she marries you!"

Ira looked at Diane again and smiled. "You were right, Sparrow. He's changed my mind. Let's go home." He stood up and offered her a hand. She took it. Together they walked away from the raving old man, went out of the huge pile of carved and tessellated stone, got into their car and drove off.

"So simple," Ira marveled, leaving the clanging gates behind. "So easy. All I have to do is marry you, and you'll be poverty-stricken. Down to your last million or so. What was it, now, you wanted so much that you had to marry me? Not security, I guess."

She leaned against him and kissed the inch or so of neck above his collar. "I wanted to set my children a good example."

"What children?"

"Excuse me. I should have said our children."

"That's better. We'll start right away."

"We already have."

He slowed and stopped the car and drew her into his arms. In a moment he caught his breath, enough to ask: "When?"

"I'm not positive, but maybe it was in Charlotte Amalie. That's when I forgot my pills. On purpose. Anyway, he'll be here in time to join us on our trip to Alaska."

"Oh, God." He put his face into her hair and nuzzled. "Are you frightened?"

"No. It'll be fine," she said softly. "After all, it's part of our job. We're helping to save an endangered species."

He raised his head and tipped up her chin, looking into her eyes. "What in the world are you talking about? What species?"

She smiled. "Human beings. Maybe we don't deserve it, but I'm prejudiced. I want to try."

Holding her tightly, Ira began to laugh. "Why not? If that's what you want to do, I want to help. I have a feeling we'll be good at it."

HARLEQUIN *Temptation*

Lovers Apart

FOUR CONTROVERSIAL STORIES! FOUR DYNAMITE AUTHORS!

In this new Temptation miniseries, four modern couples are separated by jobs, distance or emotional barriers and must work to find a resolution.

Don't miss the LOVERS APART miniseries—four special Temptation books—one per month beginning in January 1991. Look for...

LAP-1

Coming soon
to an easy chair near you.

FIRST CLASS is Harlequin's armchair travel plan for the incurably romantic. You'll visit a different dreamy destination every month from January through December without ever packing a bag. No jet lag, no expensive air fares and *no* lost luggage. Just First Class Harlequin Romance reading, featuring exotic settings from Tasmania to Thailand, from Egypt to Australia, and more.

FIRST CLASS romantic excursions guaranteed! Start your world tour in January. Look for the special **FIRST CLASS** destination on selected Harlequin Romance titles—there's a new one every month.

NEXT DESTINATION:
THAILAND

 Harlequin Books

JTR2

This February,
Harlequin helps you
celebrate the most
romantic day of the
year with

my *Valentine* 1991

Katherine Arthur
Debbie Macomber
Leigh Michaels
Peggy Nicholson

A collection of four tender
love stories written by
celebrated Harlequin
authors.

Available wherever Harlequin books are sold.

VAL

You'll flip . . . your pages won't!
Read paperbacks *hands-free* with

Book Mate · I

The perfect "mate" for all your romance paperbacks

Traveling • Vacationing • At Work • In Bed • Studying • Cooking • Eating

Perfect size for all standard paperbacks, this wonderful invention makes reading a pure pleasure! Ingenious design holds paperback books OPEN and FLAT so even wind can't ruffle pages— leaves your hands free to do other things. Reinforced, wipe-clean vinyl-covered holder flexes to let you turn pages without undoing the strap . . . supports paperbacks so well, they have the strength of hardcovers!

Pages turn WITHOUT opening the strap

SEE-THROUGH STRAP

Reinforced back stays flat

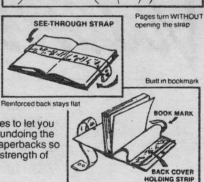

Built in bookmark

BOOK MARK

BACK COVER HOLDING STRIP

10 x 7¼ opened.
Snaps closed for easy carrying, too

Available now. Send your name, address, and zip code, along with a check or money order for just $5.95 + .75¢ for delivery (for a total of $6.70) payable to Reader Service to:

Reader Service
Bookmate Offer
3010 Walden Avenue
P.O. Box 1396
Buffalo, N.Y. 14269-1396

Offer not available in Canada
*New York residents add appropriate sales tax.

BM-GR